Enid Blyton's

ROUND THE CLOCK STORIES

Enid Blyton's

ROUND THE CLOCK STORIES

PRINTED IN GREAT BRITAIN
DEAN & **SON Ltd.**
52 54 Southwark St. LONDON SE1 1UA
TRADE MARK

© Enid Blyton 1963

MADE AND PRINTED IN GREAT BRITAIN BY PURNELL AND SONS LTD.
PAULTON (AVON) AND LONDON
603 03255 9

CONTENTS

The Little Singing Kettle

MISTER CURLY was a small pixie who lived all by himself in Twisty Cottage. His cottage stood at the end of the Village of Ho, and was always very neatly kept. It had blue and yellow curtains at the windows and blue and yellow flowers in the garden, so you can guess how pretty and trim it was.

Mister Curly was mean. He was the meanest pixie that ever lived, but he always pretended to be very generous indeed. If he had a bag of peppermints he never let anyone see it, but put it straight into his pocket till he got home. And if he met any of the other pixies he would pull a long face and say:

"If only I had a bag of sweets I would offer you one."

"Never mind," the others said. "It's nice of you to think of it!"

And they went off, saying what a nice, generous creature Mister Curly was!

Now one day, as Mister Curly was walking home along Dimity Lane, where the trees met overhead, so that it was just like walking in a green tunnel, he saw a queer fellow in front of him. This was a Humpy Goblin, and he carried a great many saucepans, kettles and pans all slung down his back, round his shoulders and over his chest.

They made a great noise as he walked, but louder than the noise was the Humpy Goblin's voice. He sang all the time in a voice like a cracked bell.

" Do you want a saucepan, kettle or pan?
If you do, here's the Goblin Man!

The Humpy Goblin with his load
Of pots and pans is down the road,
Hie, hie, hie, here's the Goblin Man,
Do you want a saucepan, kettle or pan?"

Now Mister Curly badly wanted a new kettle, because his own had a hole in it and the water leaked over his stove each day, making a funny hissing noise. So he ran after the Goblin Man and called him. The Humpy Goblin turned round and grinned. He was a cheerful fellow, always pleased to see anybody.

"I want a good little kettle, nice and cheap," said Curly.

"I've just the one for you," said Humpy, and he pointed to a

bright little kettle on his back. Curly looked at it.

"How much is it?" he asked.

"Sixpence," said the Goblin. This was quite cheap, but mean old Curly wasn't going to give sixpence for the kettle. He pretended to be shocked at the price, and then he gave a huge sigh.

"Oh, I'm not rich enough to pay all that," he said sadly. "I can only pay threepence."

"Oh, no," said Humpy firmly. "Threepence isn't enough. You must pay sixpence."

Well, they stood and talked to one another for a long time, one saying sixpence and the other saying threepence, until at last the Humpy Goblin laughed in Curly's face and walked off jingling all his kettles and pans.

"You're a mean old stick!" he called after Curly. "I'm not going to sell you anything! Good-bye, Mister Mean!"

Off he went and soon began to sing his song again. Curly heard him.

> "Do you want a saucepan, kettle or pan?
> If you do, here's the Goblin Man!"

Curly stood and watched him angrily. Then he started walking, too. He had to follow the Goblin Man because that was the way home to Twisty Cottage. But he took care not to follow too close, for he was afraid that Humpy might call something rude after him.

It was a hot day and the Goblin was tired. After a while he thought he would sit down in the hedge and rest. So down he sat—and it wasn't more than a minute before he was sound asleep and snoring! Curly heard him and knew he must be asleep. A naughty thought slipped into his head.

"I wonder if I could take that kettle from him whilst he's asleep! I could leave threepence beside him to pay for it. How cross he would be when he woke up to find that I had got the kettle for threepence after all!"

He crept up to the Humpy Goblin. He certainly was sound asleep, with his mouth so wide open that it was a good thing there wasn't anything above his head that could drop into it. Curly carefully undid the little shining kettle without making even a clink of noise. Then he put three bright pennies on the grass beside the Goblin, and ran off, chuckling to himself for being so smart.

He soon reached home. He filled the little kettle with water and put it on the fire. It really was a dear little thing, and it boiled very quickly indeed, sending a spurt of steam out of the spout almost before Curly had got out the teapot to make the tea.

Just as he was sitting down to enjoy a cup of tea and a piece of cake, someone walked up his garden path and looked in at the door. It was the Humpy Goblin. When he saw that Curly had the kettle on the fire, he grinned all over his face.

" So you've got it ! " he said. " Well, much good may it do you ! Kettle, listen to me ! Teach Mister Curly the lesson he needs ! Ho, ho, Curly, keep the kettle ! I don't want it ! "

Laughing and skipping, the Goblin went down the path again. Curly felt a bit uncomfortable. What was he laughing like that for ?

" Oh, he just tried to frighten me and make me think something nasty would happen," said Curly to himself. " Silly old Goblin ! "

He cleared away his cup and saucer, and filled up the kettle again. He was washing up the dirty dishes when a knock came at his door, and Dame Pitapat looked in.

" I say, Curly, could you let me have a little tea ? I've emptied my tin and it's such a long way to the shops."

Now Curly had a whole tin full, but he wasn't going to let Dame Pitapat have any. He ran to the dresser and took down a tin he knew was empty.

" Yes, certainly, Dame Pitapat," he said, " you shall have some of my tea. Oh, dear ! The tin's empty ! What a pity ! You could have had half of it if only I'd had any, but I must have used it all up ! "

Dame Pitapat looked at the empty tin. Then she turned to go.

" I'm sorry I bothered you, Curly," she said. " It was kind of you to say I could have had half, if only you'd had any tea."

Then a funny thing happened. The little kettle on the stove sent out a big spurt of steam and began to sing a shrill song.

> " *Mister Curly has plenty of tea !*
> *He's just as mean as a pixie can be !*
> *Look in the tin on the left of the shelf*
> *And see what a lot he has for himself !* "

Then the kettle took another breath and shouted, " Mean old thing ! Stingy old thing ! Oooooh, look at him ! "

Dame Pitapat was so astonished that she stood gaping for quite a minute. She couldn't think where the song came from. She had no idea it was the kettle on the stove. But Curly knew it was, and he was so angry and ashamed that he could have cried.

Dame Pitapat went to the shelf and took down the tin that

stood on the left. She opened it, and sure
enough, it was full to the brim of tea.

"Oh, look at this!" she said.
"Well, Curly, you said I could
have half of any tea you had, so I
shall take you at your word. Thanks
very much." She emptied half the
tea out into the tin she had brought
and went out of the cottage, looking round curiously to see if she
could spy who had sung that song
about Curly. But she didn't think
of looking at the kettle, of course.

Curly was so angry with the kettle
that he decided to beat it with a
stick. But before he could do that
someone poked his head in at the
window and called him.

"Mister Curly! Will you lend me your umbrella, please?
I've lost mine and it's raining."

It was little Capers, the pixie who lived next door. He was
always lending Curly things, and now he had come to borrow
something himself. But Curly was in a very bad temper.

"My umbrella's lost too," he said. "I'm so sorry, Capers.
You could have it if only I had it myself, but it's gone."

"Oh, well, never mind," said Capers. "It's nice of you to
say you would have lent it to me."

Before he could go the shining kettle gave a tiny hop on
the stove and began to sing again.

> "Mister Curly has got an umbrella,
> He's such a mean and stingy fella,
> He says he hasn't got one at all
> But just you go and look in the hall!"

Then it took another breath and began to shout again at the top of its steamy voice, " Mean old thing ! Stingy old thing ! Oooooh, look at him ! "

Capers was so surprised to hear this song that he nearly fell in at the window. He stared at Curly, who was looking as black as thunder and as red as a beetroot. Then Capers looked through the kitchen door into the tiny hall—and sure enough Curly's green umbrella stood there.

Capers jumped in at the window and fetched the umbrella. He waved it at Curly.

" You said I could have it if only you had got it ! " he cried. " Here it is, so I'll borrow it ! Many thanks ! "

He ran off and left Curly nearly crying with rage. The pixie caught up a stick and ran to beat the kettle—but that small kettle was far too quick for him ! It rose up in the air and put itself high up on a shelf for safety. Then it poured just a drop of boiling water on to Curly's hand, which made the pixie dance and shout with pain.

" You wait till I get you ! " cried Curly, shaking his stick.

Someone knocked at his front door. Curly opened it. Rag and Tag, the two gnomes, stood there smiling.

" Mister Curly, we are collecting pennies for poor Mister Tumble whose house was burnt down yesterday," they said. " You are so generous that we thought you would be sure to give us one."

Curly knew that there was no money in his pockets, so he pulled them inside out quickly, saying, "Oh yes, you shall have whatever money I have, Rag and Tag. Goodness,

there's none in this pocket—and none in that! How unfortunate! I haven't any pennies to give you, and I should have been *so* pleased to have let you have all I had."

"Well, that's very nice of you to say so," said Rag and Tag. "Never mind. Thank you very much for *trying* to be generous!"

Before they could go, that little kettle was singing again, spurting out great clouds of steam as it did so!

> "*Although he says he hasn't any,*
> *Curly's got a silver penny!*
> *Look in his purse on the table there*
> *And take the money he well can spare!*"

Then, taking another breath, the kettle shouted with all its might, "Mean old thing! Stingy old thing! Oooooh, look at him!"

Rag and Tag stared all round the kitchen to see where the voice came from, but they couldn't see anyone but Curly. It couldn't be the pixie singing, surely! No, he looked too angry and ashamed to sing anything!

The gnomes saw the purse lying on the table and they ran

for it. Inside was a silver sixpence. They took it and put it into their box.

"Well, Curly," they said, "you said we might have any pennies you had, if you'd had any—and you have, so we'll take this silver one. Good-bye!"

Out they went, giggling together, wondering who it was in the cottage that had given Curly away.

As for Curly, he was so angry that he caught up a jug of milk and flung it straight at the kettle, which was still high up on the shelf. Crash! The kettle hopped aside and the jug broke in a dozen pieces against the wall behind. The milk spilt and dripped on to Curly's head. Then the kettle began to laugh. How it laughed! It was a funny, wheezy laugh, but you can't think how angry it made Curly!

He took up a hammer and flung that at the kettle too—but once more it slipped to one side, and oh, dear me, smash went a lovely big jar of plum jam up on the shelf. It all splashed down on to Curly, so what with milk and jam he was a fine sight. The kettle nearly killed itself with laughing. It almost fell off the shelf.

Curly went and washed himself under the tap. He felt frightened. What was he going to do with that awful singing kettle? He must get rid of it somehow or it would tell everyone the most dreadful tales about him.

"I'll wait till to-night," thought Curly. "Then, when it's asleep, I'll take it and throw it away."

So he took no more notice of the kettle, and as no other

visitors came that day the kettle was fairly quiet—except that sometimes it would suddenly shout, " Mean old thing ! Stingy old thing ! Oooooooh, look at him ! " Then Curly would almost jump out of his skin with fright, and glare at the kettle angrily.

At nine o'clock Curly went to bed. The kettle hopped down to the stove and went to sleep. Curly waited for a little while and then he crept out of bed. He went to the stove and took hold of the kettle. Ah, he had it now ! The kettle woke up and shouted, but Curly had it by the handle. The water in it was no longer hot, so that it could not hurt Curly.

The pixie hurried outside with the kettle and went to the bottom of his garden. There was a rubbish-heap there and the pixie stuffed the struggling kettle right into the middle. He left it there and went back delighted. He climbed into bed and fell asleep.

But at midnight something woke him by tapping at the window.

" Let me in ! " cried a voice. " Let me in ! I'm dirty and I want washing ! "

" That's that horrid kettle ! " thought Curly, in a fright. " Well, it can go on tapping ! I won't let it in ! "

But the kettle tapped and tapped and at last it flung itself hard against the glass, broke it and came in through the hole ! It went over to Curly's bed and stood itself there.

" Wash me ! " it said. " I'm dirty and smelly. You shouldn't have put me on that nasty rubbish-heap ! "

" Get out of my nice clean bed ! " cried Curly angrily. " Look what a mess you are making ! "

But the kettle wouldn't get off, and in the end the angry pixie had to get up and wash the kettle till it was clean again. Then he banged it down on the stove and left it.

Next day the kettle sang songs about him again, and Curly kept hearing it shout, " Mean old fellow ! Stingy old fellow !

Ooooooh, look at him!" till he was tired of it. So many people had heard about the strange things happening in the pixie's cottage that all day long visitors came to ask for different things, and poor Curly was nearly worried out of his life.

"I'll drown that kettle in my well to-night!" he thought. So once more he took the kettle when it was asleep and threw it down the well. Splash! Ha, it wouldn't get out of there in a hurry!

But about three o'clock in the morning there came a tap-tap-tap at the window, which had now been mended. It was the kettle back again!

"Curly! Let me in! I'm c-c-c-c-cold and w-wet! Let me in!"

Curly was afraid his window would be broken again, so he jumped out of bed and let in the shivering kettle. To his horror it crept into bed with him and wouldn't go away!

"It was cold and wet in the well!" said the kettle. "Warm me, Curly!"

So Curly had to warm the kettle, and how angry he was! It was so uncomfortable to sleep with a kettle, especially one that kept sticking its sharp spout into him. But he had to put up with it. In the morning he put the kettle back on the stove and started to think hard whilst he had his breakfast.

"I can't get rid of that kettle," he said to himself. "And while it's here it's sure to sing horrid things about me every time anyone comes to borrow something. I wonder what it would do if I let people have what they ask for? I'll try and see."

So when Mother Homey came and begged for a bit of soap because she had run out of it and the shops were closed that afternoon Curly gave her a whole new piece without making any excuse at all. Mother Homey was surprised and delighted.

"Thank you so much," she said. "You're a kind soul, Curly."

The kettle said nothing at all. Not a single word. As for Curly, he suddenly felt very nice inside. It was lovely to give somebody something. It made him feel warm and kind. He made up his mind to do it again if he felt nice the next time— and to see if that wretched kettle said anything.

He soon found that the kettle said never a word unless he was mean or untruthful—and he found, too, that it was lovely to be kind and to give things away; it was nice even to lend them.

"I've been horrid and nasty," thought Curly to himself. "I'll turn over a new leaf and try to be different. And that old kettle can say what it likes! Anyway, it boils very quickly and makes a lovely pot of tea."

Very soon the kettle found little to say, for Curly became kind and generous. Once or twice he forgot, but as soon as he heard the kettle beginning to speak he quickly remembered, and the kettle stopped its song.

And one day who should peep in at the door but the Humpy Goblin, grinning all over his face as usual.

"Hallo, Curly!" he said. "How did you like the kettle? Was it cheap for threepence? I've come to take it back, if you want to get rid of it. It was a mean trick to play you, really, but I think you deserved it!"

Curly looked at the smiling Goblin. Then he took his purse

from his pocket and found three pennies. He held them out
to the Humpy Goblin.

"Here you are," he said. "You wanted sixpence for the
kettle and I was mean enough to leave you only threepence.
Here's the other threepence."

"But—but—don't you want to give me back the kettle?"
asked Humpy in surprise. "I left a horrid singing spell in it."

"Yes, I know," said Curly. "But I deserved it. I'm different
now. I like the kettle too—we're great friends. I try to be
kind now, so the kettle doesn't sing nasty things about me.
It just hums nice, friendly little songs."

" Well, well, well, wonders will never end ! " said the Goblin Man, astonished. " Don't bother about the other threepence, Curly. I don't want it."

" Well, if you won't take it, let me offer you a cup of tea made from water boiled in the singing kettle," said Curly. Humpy was even more astonished to hear the pixie being so kind, but he sat down at the table in delight.

Then he and Curly had a cup of tea each and a large slice of ginger cake—and they talked together and found that they liked one another very much indeed.

So now Mister Curly and the Humpy Goblin are the very greatest friends, and the little singing kettle hums its loudest when it boils water for their tea. You should just hear it !

The Little Brown Duck

ON THE stream that ran between the buttercup fields two wild ducks had a nest. The drake was a most beautiful fellow, dressed in blues and greens; but his mate was a little brown duck. She kept close to the nest and sat on her eggs happily. The drake swam about and quacked cheerfully to his mate every now and again.

The only person that knew about the two wild ducks was Benny. He had seen the nest one day as he was walking along the bank, but he didn't tell anyone at all. It was Benny's secret.

"I do hope no one finds the nest," thought Benny. "Oh, I do hope the eggs hatch out into tiny ducklings. I shall see them then. The brown duck doesn't seem to mind me looking. She knows I won't hurt her."

The eggs hatched. Seven downy ducklings lay in the nest of reeds by the stream-side. Benny loved them. They did look so quaint with their big beaks and fluffy feathers.

Then one day the mother duck took them all for a swim. Benny was there to see them. Each little downy duckling tumbled into the water and swam hard as soon as it was there. They swam after their mother in a long line. The father duck, the drake, swam a good way ahead to make sure that the way was clear.

Benny went to see the ducks every day. They grew and they grew. Nobody knew about them until August Bank Holiday came. Then a motor-coach brought some trippers from the towns; and three big boys, wandering along by the stream-side, saw the little brown duck with her brood of ducklings.

And what do you suppose they did ? Well, you will hardly believe it, but they picked up stones and began to throw them at the little duck family. The little brown duck quacked in alarm. Her ducklings swam close to her in terror. The stones fell thick and fast around. One little duckling was hit, and quacked in pain and fright.

And just then Benny came along. He was only a little boy ; but when he saw those three big boys throwing stones at the little duck family, he forgot all about being small.

" Hi ! Stop that ! " he shouted at the top of his voice. " How dare you ! Stop throwing stones at once."

The boys stopped. They stared round at Benny.

" Pooh ! It's only a little boy," they said, and they began to throw stones again. " Quack, quack, quack ! " said the ducks in terror.

Benny didn't know what to do. He suddenly ran at one of the big boys and butted his head against him.

The boy lost his balance and fell headlong into the stream— splash ! Benny butted the next boy, and, taken by surprise, in he went too ! The third boy was full of fear, for he thought his friends would be drowned, but Benny knew the water was not deep.

"If you frighten those ducks that never did you or anyone any harm, you deserve to be frightened yourselves," shouted Benny.

The boys climbed out, dripping wet. They were just about to catch Benny and whip him when someone called from the field gate. "Hi! The motor-coach is going soon. Hurry, or you'll miss it."

The boys rushed off. Benny was trembling, and he sat down on the bank. He had quite expected to be hit by all the big boys. The mother duck brought her ducklings to the rushes as soon as she saw that the big boys had gone. Benny leaned over to see them. He picked out of the water the little duckling that had been hit. Its tiny wing was bruised, but Benny thought it would heal. He put the trembling creature back.

"Quack, quack, quack!" said the mother duck gratefully. She knew quite well that Benny had helped her.

Now when Benny's birthday came, he had a great surprise. Uncle Harry gave him a beautiful sailing-ship. Benny was simply delighted.

"Now I can go down to the river and sail it every day," he said. So down to the river he went. The little stream on which the ducks nested ran into the river, but Benny was so interested in his ship that he forgot all about the little duck family for a time. He sailed his ship every day and loved to see it bobbing up and down on the waves.

And then one afternoon a dreadful thing happened. Benny was sailing his ship on the river, when he suddenly dropped the string into the water. The wind blew the ship strongly, and it sailed away by itself into the middle of the river. Benny couldn't guide it or pull it in, because the string was gone.

"Oh, my ship, my beautiful ship," groaned the little boy. "It will float away down the river and be lost, and

some other boy will get it and have it. Oh, whatever shall I do?"

He looked about to see if there was anyone near who might help him; but no, not a single person was in sight. The ship was as good as lost. There it sailed, down the river; it would soon be gone.

But what was this? A little brown head poked out of the nearby rushes, and a small brown body followed. It was the little brown duck. Her babies were all grown now and had gone away to look after themselves, but the little brown duck still swam about the stream and the river she loved.

She saw Benny's boat and somehow knew how unhappy he was. She swam after the ship—how she swam! She paddled her strong legs fast, fast, faster.

"Oh! She's going after my boat. Oh, the kind, clever little duck!" cried Benny, nearly falling into the river with joy and delight. "Oh, she's almost got it—she's up to it—good little duck, good little duck!"

The little brown duck had reached the ship. She tried to stop it going down the river, but it slipped round her and went on again. Then she caught sight of the string that drifted through the water behind it. She darted at it with her beak, and caught it. The ship stopped and came round a bit. The duck tugged at the string. The ship jerked.

"Come, little duck, come!" shouted Benny. "Bring the string to me. Oh, you clever little duck!"

The duck swam over the water to Benny, holding the string in her mouth. The ship followed her, rocking up and down. Benny reached out as soon as the duck was near enough. He took the string gently from the little bird's beak, and pulled his precious ship in to shore.

"Thank you very much indeed," he said to the little brown duck. "You were a good friend to me to-day. I suppose you remembered how I saved you from those big boys some time ago."

"Quack, quack, quack!" said the little wild duck, which meant, "Of course I remembered. One good turn deserves another!"

Then off she swam, bobbing up and down happily.

You never know when a kindness is going to come back to you, do you?

The Pixie who Killed the Moon

THERE was once upon a time a silly little pixie called Big Eyes. He never stopped to think about anything at all, and he always believed every single thing he was told.

When a chestnut fell down on his head one night he ran away in terror, shouting at the top of his voice:

"A star has fallen on me! A star has fallen on me!"

The other pixies, who had seen the chestnut fall, laughed at him. "Catch it, then!" they cried. "It is shining in your hair."

Big Eyes leant over a pool and, sure enough, he saw a star shining, as he thought, in his hair.

He took a comb and combed all night, but he couldn't find the star. I'm not surprised, either. Are you?

Another time he heard a nightingale singing, and he wanted to take it home to live with him, but it wouldn't come. It sat in its bush and sang beautifully, and took no notice of Big Eyes.

"Build a fence round the bush!" said the other pixies. "Then he can't get away, Big Eyes."

So Big Eyes gathered a great deal of bracken and weaved a tight little fence all round the bush.

The nightingale watched him with great interest. "What's that for, Big Eyes?" he asked.

"Wait and see," said Big Eyes.

So the nightingale waited. When the fence was finished Big Eyes jumped over it and laughed.

"Ho! ho!" he cried. "Now I've got you, my little nightingale! Come home with me and live in my cottage.

You shall have wild strawberries for breakfast, and I will polish your beak every morning for you."

"No, not I," said the nightingale.

"But you must," said Big Eyes.

"Trilla—trilla—trilla!" sang the nightingale, mockingly. "You cannot make me!"

"Yes, I can!" said Big Eyes. "I have built a fence all round you, and you cannot escape me. I shall catch you and take you home with me."

"Catch me, then!" cried the nightingale, and spread his wings. He flew straight up and over the fence and disappeared, singing, into the wood.

All the watching pixies laughed as Big Eyes stared in dismay.

"Why don't you think, Big Eyes?" they cried. "You knew that a nightingale could fly! Why didn't you *think*?"

Big Eyes was upset, but he didn't try to mend his ways—not he! It was too much bother, and *he* wasn't going to try.

Now one day a child went through the wood in which Big Eyes lived. She carried a big yellow balloon, and it floated prettily behind her. Suddenly there came a great gust of wind and—puff!—the string was blown out of her hand and the balloon went sailing gaily away into the wood. It floated through the air for a long time, until it came to the place where Big Eyes was having his dinner.

It landed just by him and stayed there with its string caught in a bramble bush. Big Eyes jumped up in fright, for he had heard no noise and hadn't seen the balloon coming.

Crash! went his plate, and Big Eyes fled through the wood, howling with fright.

"What's the matter?" cried everyone.

"The moon's fallen down by me!" wept Big Eyes. "The big yellow moon! It came whilst I was eating my dinner, and almost killed me!"

The pixies laughed loudly and went to see what it was.

"Isn't he a silly?" they said, when they saw it was only a balloon. "He always cries before he's hurt. Let's pretend it *is* the moon, and see what he'll do!"

So they pretended it was the moon, and Big Eyes told them again and again how it had nearly fallen on his head and killed him.

"It was a shame to give you such a fright!" said the pixies.

"I should punish the moon if I were you!"

"How?" asked Big Eyes.

"Well, prick it with a pin!" said the pixies. "That will make the moon squeal out and punish it finely. But wait until it is asleep in the hot sun!"

So Big Eyes waited. He got a very long pin and hid himself in the bushes near by. Then, when the sun was high in the sky at mid-day and he thought the moon was sleeping, he crept up to it.

With a trembling hand he stuck the pin into the fat yellow balloon.

BANG! It burst with a tremendous pop, and Big Eyes was

nearly frightened to death. All
the watching pixies were, too,
and tumbled head over heels in
the bushes.

Big Eyes fled for his life. He
jumped down a rabbit-hole and
sat there trembling.

"Oh dear! Oh dear!" he
said. "I've killed the moon!
It's burst all to nothing! I've
killed the moon! What *will* the
Fairy Queen say to me? Oh dear! Oh dear, dear!"

The more he thought about it the more he shivered and
shook.

"I've killed it dead!" he said. "Bang! It went like that—
and all because I pricked it with a pin! How was *I* to know
that would kill the moon? And now we won't be able to
dance in the moonlight any more!"

All that day and all that night, and the next day, too, Big
Eyes sat in his hole, sad and sorry.

"I didn't mean to," he wept. "It was only to punish the
moon for frightening me. I hope the Queen won't be
angry!"

When the evening of the next day came poor Big Eyes
determined to go to the Queen and confess what he had
done.

So he crept out of his hole and made his way to the glade
where the Fairy Queen held her court. She was there, and
welcomed the trembling little pixie.

"What's the matter, Big Eyes?" she asked.

"Oh, Your Majesty!" wept Big Eyes. "I've done a
dreadful thing! I've killed the moon!"

"Killed the moon!" said the Queen in astonishment.
"You can't have done that, Big Eyes!"

"But I *did*!" said Big Eyes. "I pricked it with a pin and it went BANG!—like that, and died!"

The Fairy Queen laughed. Then she took Big Eyes by the arm and pointed to a hill in the distance.

"See!" she said. "What is that peeping over the hill yonder?"

Big Eyes looked. It was the big round moon, yellow and bright, rising slowly above the hill.

He stared in astonishment. So he hadn't killed it, after all!

"The other pixies have made fun of you instead of helping you!" said the Queen. "They will be punished. And you, Big Eyes, you must use your brains and think. Go back to the pixie school and learn all you can. Then you will never be so silly again!"

Big Eyes was so glad to think that he hadn't really killed the moon that he went home singing all the way. And I'm sure you will be glad to know that he was never so stupid again!

Old Bufo the Toad

OLD Bufo was a toad, fat, brown, and ugly. The only beautiful thing about him was his pair of bright, copper eyes. They were like two shining jewels.

Bufo was not allowed in Fairyland. The fairies said he really was much too ugly. He frightened them. So Bufo lived in our world, under a big stone by the streamside. He had a little shop under his stone, and there he worked hard all day long.

What do you think he made? Guess! Yes—toadstools! He was very clever indeed at making these. First he would make a nice sturdy stump, then a pretty curved cap-like top, and then underneath he sewed dozens of tiny frills. So you can see he was a busy fellow.

Now one day the Queen of Fairyland went on a long journey. She visited the Moon. She visited the Land of Dreams. And she visited our world too. She went with six servants, and she wore no crown, for she did not want to be known as she passed here and there.

She called herself Dame Silverwings, and travelled about quite safely in her silver coach, drawn by two white mice.

One day she heard that someone was chasing after her coach to catch her. It was the wizard Tall-Hat. He had found out that Dame Silverwings was no other than the Fairy Queen herself, and he thought that it would be a fine thing to catch her and take her prisoner. He would not let her go until he had been paid ten sacks of gold. Aha! How rich he would be!

A blackbird warned the Queen that Tall-Hat was after her. She hurried on her way—and then alas ! a fog came down—and she was lost ! On and on went her little white mice, dragging the carriage, but they did not know at all where they were going. When the fog cleared, they were quite lost.

The Queen stepped from her carriage. She was by a stream in a wood. No one seemed to be about at all.

"Is anyone living near here?" she called in her bird-like voice. She listened for an answer—and one came. It was the voice of Bufo, the old toad, that answered. His home was under the big stone nearby. He crawled out and croaked loudly :

"Yes—I, Bufo the toad, live here. Pray come and shelter, if you wish."

The Queen and her six servants looked at Bufo in surprise,

but when they saw his beautiful coppery eyes they trusted him and went to his stone. The Queen was surprised to see such a pretty and neat little shop under the stone—and when she saw the stools she was delighted.

"May I sit down on one of these dear little stools?" she asked. "Oh, how nice they are! Just the right height, too! I would like to rest here awhile."

"Then pray rest on my toadstools," said Bufo. "I have enough for all of you. And let me offer you each a glass of honey-dew."

The kindly old toad fussed over his visitors and made them very welcome. The Queen was glad to rest on the quaint toadstool after her long ride.

"I am Dame Silverwings," she said. "Which is the quickest way to Fairyland from here?"

"Do you see this stream?" said Bufo. "Well, on the other side lies Fairyland. There is a bridge a little farther on."

"Oh, we shall soon be home then," said the fairy, very pleased. But just as she said that she heard the noise of wings and, peeping from the stone, she saw to her horror the Tall-Hat Wizard himself, looking all round for her. He passed by, and she knew he had gone to the bridge to guard it so that she could not cross to Fairyland.

She began to weep. Bufo the toad could not bear to see her tears, and he begged her to tell him what was the matter. As soon as he heard about Tall-Hat guarding the bridge to Fairyland, he laughed.

"We can easily trick him," he said. "You shall cross the stream another way."

"But there are no boats here," said the Queen.

"I have something that will do just as well," said Bufo. He took up one of his toadstools and turned it upside down. "Look," he said, "if I put this into the water upside down, you can sit on the little frills and hold on to the stalk, then the

toadstool will float you across the stream safely. I have seven fine toadstools I can spare for you."

In the greatest delight the Queen and her servants hurried down to the water with the toadstools. They let them float there upside down. Then one by one they climbed on to their toadstools, waved good-bye to old Bufo, and floated to the opposite side. Once there they were safe!

Tall-Hat waited by the bridge for six weeks—and then heard that the Queen had been safely back in Fairyland all that time. How angry he was! And how Bufo the toad laughed when he heard him go by, shouting and raging! He didn't know that Bufo was peeping at him from under his big stone.

Bufo got such a surprise when he knew that the little fairy he had helped was the Fairy Queen herself. She sent him a gold watch and chain to wear, and an order for as many toadstools as he and his friends could make. "They will do so nicely for our parties in the woods," she said.

So now Bufo and his family make toadstools all day long, and stand them about in the woods for the little folk to sit on, or to use for tables at their parties. And Bufo is allowed in Fairyland, and has a grand time at the palace once a month when he goes to tea with the Queen herself. Nobody thinks he is ugly now, for they always look at his glowing eyes. Have you seen them? You haven't? Well, just look at them next time you see an old toad hopping along.

And don't forget to look at the dear little frills Bufo puts under every toadstool, will you?

The Boy who Pulled Tails

THERE was once a boy called Bobby who lived with his mother and father in a small cottage by a thick forest. His father worked at a farm nearby, and Bobby often used to go with him to see the young calves or the new yellow chickens.

But animals and birds didn't like Bobby. He always pulled ir tails. He just did it to tease them, and they hated it. It ..ightened them. Bobby didn't care—he just went on pulling them.

He pulled the tail of Whiskers, his mother's cat, too. He often caught hold of the long, shaggy tail of Bingo, his father's old dog, and made him yelp with pain. He pulled the pony's tail, and he even pulled the pretty, drooping tail of Doodle-doo, the fine cock that lived with the brown hens in the yard at the back of the cottage.

Wasn't he silly? He just did it to annoy the animals, because he wasn't really a cruel boy. He never forgot to feed his rabbit, and he always saw that the dog had plenty of water to drink. His mother was quite upset about his silly trick.

"One of these days something will happen to make you sorry you pull tails so much!" she said. "I'm ashamed of you, Bobby."

But Bobby only laughed and ran out of the back door, pulling the cat's tail as he went.

And then one day something *did* happen! Bobby went for a long walk and took his lunch with him in a basket. It was a lovely sunny day, and he thought he would look for wild strawberries in the forest. He followed the little path that led

37

into the wood and whistled gaily as he went. He hunted here and there for wild strawberries but couldn't see any at all.

"Perhaps there are some further in," he thought, and he followed another path, a winding one that led between the big, shady trees, towards the heart of the forest.

Bobby very soon found plenty of strawberries under the trees, and he ate dozens of them. They were little and very sweet. And then he suddenly saw someone else gathering them.

It was a little bent man, dressed in a green suit. His shoes were green too, and had long pointed toes. He carried a green basket and in it he put the wild strawberries. He had a beard that reached right down to the ground.

Bobby stared at him in surprise.

"It must be a gnome!" he thought, in excitement. "I wonder where he lives. I'll hide behind this tree and watch where he goes."

So he hid himself and watched the busy gnome. When the little man's basket was full he set off through the trees at a jog-trot. Bobby followed, feeling most excited.

The path widened out and suddenly ran into a lane. At the far end of the lane stood a tiny cottage, with blue windows and door and cream walls. The gnome went into the cottage and shut the door.

A red wall ran round the garden, and on it sat a big black cat with red whiskers. Bobby thought he must be a gnome cat, he looked so queer. His tail hung down over the wall, and, of course, you can guess what Bobby did.

He caught hold of the cat's long tail and pulled it!

And then a dreadful and most surprising thing happened. The tail came off! Yes, right off in Bobby's hand. The cat gave a frightened yell and ran to the house. It jumped in at an open window, mewing loudly.

Bobby stood there with the tail in his hand, almost as frightened as the cat. Suddenly the door of the house flew open and out rushed the gnome in a fearful rage.

He danced about on the path, shouting and yelling at Bobby.

"You wicked boy! You horrid, cruel, unkind boy! You've pulled my cat's tail off!"

"I didn't mean to," said Bobby, the tears coming into his eyes. "Truly I didn't."

"You're always pulling tails!" shouted the gnome,

shaking his fist at Bobby. "All sorts of animals and birds complain about you. You're a nuisance, a great big NUISANCE!"

"What shall I do with this tail?" asked Bobby. "Can you put it back again on your cat?"

"No, I can't. Cinders, my cat, will grow a new one in a year," said the gnome. "The tails of gnome cats come off very easily, and you ought to have known that."

"Well, I didn't," said Bobby. "I wouldn't have pulled it if I had known that."

"You can have Cinders' tail for yourself," suddenly said the gnome. He snatched the tail from Bobby's hand and threw it at him. It stuck on the little boy's back—and oh, my goodness me, it grew there! Bobby had a long cat's tail behind him.

The gnome began to laugh. How he laughed! He held his sides and laughed till the tears poured down his cheeks. Then he took a whistle from his pocket and blew on it. From many little cottages near poured a troop of pixies, brownies and gnomes, and when the gnome explained to them what had happened they began laughing too.

But Bobby was crying. He wanted to ask the gnome how he could get rid of the cat's tail, but everyone was laughing so loudly that he couldn't make himself heard. So he turned and ran away as fast as he could, trying to get away from the sound of the merry fairy laughter.

He came to the edge of the forest, and sat down to think

about things. He tugged at the tail. It was certainly quite fast on him. He couldn't get it off, and it hurt him to pull it. What a dreadful thing! He'd have to go home like that and tell his father and mother what had happened.

He walked slowly home, the black tail swishing behind him. He was a very sad little boy. At last he reached his cottage, and went in. His mother looked up and when she saw the long black tail she cried out in astonishment:

" What's that you've got?"

Then Bobby told her, and she looked very grave.

" I told you something would happen to you one day if you went on pulling tails," she said. " Now the best thing you can do is to stop pulling tails and hope that your own tail will gradually go."

So Bobby stopped pulling tails—but dear me, as soon as the cats, dogs, donkeys, horses, hens and ducks around saw that Bobby had a tail, they went nearly mad with delight. And they all gave it a good pull and tug whenever the little boy went by!

Then he knew what it felt like to have his tail pulled. It hurt him and made him jump. The dog used to lie in wait for him round corners, and pull his tail hard. The cat clawed it and the hens pecked it. It was dreadful to have a tail like that.

"I know now how all the birds and animals must have hated having their tails pulled," thought Bobby. "I wish I'd never been so mean. And oh, how I wish I'd never pulled that gnome-cat's tail!"

For weeks poor Bobby wore the gnome-cat's tail, and many times a day he had it pulled. He tried putting the end in one of his pockets, but it wouldn't stay there. It took itself out and waved about in the air. It wouldn't keep still, and Bobby couldn't do anything with it. He just had to put up with it.

"I'll never pull a tail again!" said Bobby, a score of times a day. "I never will!"

"Your tail doesn't seem to be going," said his mother anxiously. "I thought perhaps it would gradually disappear. I'll send a note to that little gnome and tell him you have learnt your lesson. Perhaps he will make your tail go."

So she wrote a note to tell the gnome that Bobby was a much nicer boy now, and please would he come and take the tail away. But he didn't come.

However, the next day, just as Bobby was filling up the dog's water-bowl, his tail began to twist and turn in a very peculiar manner, just as if it was trying to pull itself off. Then it suddenly shot up into the air, danced there for a moment like a short black rope and fell to the ground. Then it wriggled away like a snake and was lost to sight.

Bobby watched in amazement. He *was* glad to see it go! He ran to tell his mother and she was glad, too.

"Now mind, Bobby," she said, "don't you start pulling tails again, or that tail may come back."

"Oh, Mother, I'll never, never pull a tail again in my life!" cried Bobby. And you may be sure he never did.

As for that strange tail, nobody ever saw it again, though people do say it is waiting to grow on another boy or girl some day. I hope it won't be you or me!

The Tale of Mr. Spectacles

Tippy the gnome was sharp and sly, and no one in Apple Village liked him very much. So it was not surprising that when Dame Softly said she would have a fine garden party in her grounds she did not invite Tippy the gnome. He was most upset and annoyed about it. He sat down on his little stool, and wondered how he could go to the party, and how he could punish Dame Softly for not inviting him. Then he suddenly had a good idea.

"I'll dress up and pretend to be someone who can tell people all about themselves and say what will happen to them in the future," thought Tippy. "No one will know I am Tippy the gnome who knows all about everybody's business—and when it comes to Dame Softly's turn—ooh! won't I tell her some horrid things!"

So on the day of the garden party Tippy dressed himself up in a fine black cloak, put on a pair of dark green spectacles, and stuck a long beard on his chin. Then he marched up to Dame Softly's and asked her if she would care to let him sit in a corner of her garden and tell people's fortunes.

"I am Mister Spectacles, the Wizard," said Tippy. "I will make your party a great success. I only charge a penny a time."

"Very well," said Dame Softly. "You may sit over there on that seat in the corner. I will tell my guests about you, and perhaps come to have my fortune told too."

Down sat Tippy in delight. He waited for someone to come, and very soon up came Tickles the brownie. He paid his penny. Tippy leaned forward and pretended to look at him hard through his dark spectacles. He didn't like Tickles, because the brownie had once scolded him for being mean.

"You keep bees," said Tippy in a deep voice, "and you sell honey."

"Yes, I do," said Tickles, astonished. "Will I do well with my bees this year?"

"No," said Tippy, enjoying himself. "They will suddenly feel angry with you, and will all come and *sting* you, and *sting* you, and *sting* you . . ."

Tickles gave a yell and shot away, shouting that he would sell his bees that very day. Then up came Pip the elf, and paid his penny. Tippy scowled at him, for Pip had once spanked him for his slyness.

"You grow roses," said Tippy. "You sell the roses that you grow."

"How clever of you!" said Pip. "Will I ever make a fortune out of them?"

"Not out of your *roses*," said Tippy, an idea coming into his mind. "But underneath one of them—if you like to look—there may be a box of gold."

"Oooh!" cried Pip happily. "I'll go and dig every one of them up and find it."

Off he went, and Tippy grinned to think of Pip digging up all his precious roses for nothing. Then Mother Noddy came up and paid her penny to Tippy.

Tippy hated Mother Noddy, for she had always told him what a bad little gnome he was. So he looked at her through his spectacles, and said in a deep voice: "Dear, dear me! I can see a sad thing in store for you, old dame. One of your hens will peck you to-morrow, and you will be ill for a whole year."

Mother Noddy gave a yell and ran off shouting: "I shall set all my hens free. They shan't peck me!"

How Tippy grinned! What a time he was having! Ah—but wait and see!

Tippy sat and waited for the next person to come. It was Dame Softly, who had not invited him to her party. Aha! Tippy would make her sorry for that!

She paid her penny and sat down. Tippy stared at her through his green spectacles, and waggled his long beard about. She felt quite uncomfortable.

"Misfortune is awaiting you," said Tippy in a deep, solemn voice. "Your house will catch fire very soon."

"It's a good thing the firemen are all at my party then," said Dame Softly, pleased. "They will soon put the fire out."

"Robbers will come and steal your fine jewels," said Tippy.

"Well, as the village policeman is also at my party, the robbers will have a bad time," said Dame Softly, still more pleased.

"Is the policeman really here?" said Tippy, feeling suddenly alarmed. "I didn't know that!"

"You didn't know?" said Dame Softly in surprise. "But I thought you were Mister Spectacles, who knew everything."

Just at that moment up came Pip the elf, sobbing bitterly. "I've dug up all my lovely rose-trees," he wept, "and there was no box of gold under any of them. I have spoilt my trees— I can't sell my roses now—oh dear, oh dear! You told me a story, Mister Spectacles! And there's poor old Tickles, he's sold his beehives and all his bees for a few pence, because you said they would sting him and sting him—and I just saw Mother Noddy letting all her hens loose into the road because you said one would peck her and make her ill for a whole year.

It's a pity you ever came to this party and upset us so, especially as I've lost all my beautiful rose-trees!"

Pip began to weep bitterly. Dame Softly stared at him; then she slipped away. In a short while she brought back Mister Grab the village policeman. He sat down by Tippy and grinned.

"Well, Mister Spectacles," he said, "I hear you are a wonderful teller of fortunes. Just tell me mine, will you?"

"You—you are a policeman," said Tippy, very uncomfortable indeed.

"Right, first time!" said Mister Grab. "Now tell me the name of someone I'm going to spank this very day!"

"I d-d-don't know," stammered Tippy.

"Dear me, I thought you could tell anyone anything he asked," laughed Mister Grab. "Well, tell me this—am I going to stay at this party all the time, or am I going to leave it in the middle, and if so, shall I go alone or will anyone be with me?"

"I d-d-don't know," said poor Tippy again.

"Well, I can tell you *your* fortune," said Mister Grab, suddenly, in a very stern voice. "Your beard will come off—like that—and your spectacles will come off—like that—and lo and behold the great fortune-teller will turn into no other than Tippy the gnome—just as sly, but not so clever as usual! And Tippy will come along with me and be spanked—and he will give Pip those pennies to buy some new rose-trees—and he will soon be sorry he played such a very—stupid—trick!"

Well—Mister Grab was a *very* good fortune-teller, because everything he said came true! Poor old Tippy!

The Goblin's Pie

THERE was once a very fat goblin called Roundabout. He was fat because he was greedy. The thing he liked best of all was a pie. It didn't matter what *kind* of a pie—meat-pie, chicken-pie, veal-and-ham pie, apple-pie, plum-pie, onion-pie—he liked them all.

His friends wished he wouldn't be so greedy. They really were afraid he would burst out of his clothes one day. But Roundabout took no notice of his friends. He just went on eating and eating.

He would walk miles for a pie. Yes, really! When he heard that Dame Strawberry had baked three fine strawberry-pies one day he set out to get one. Dame Strawberry lived on Tree-Top Hill miles away, but that didn't matter. Roundabout walked and walked until he got there, and he arrived the day after to-morrow.

Well, of course, all the pies were eaten by then, except for a tiny piece left in the larder. But Roundabout ate that and said it was worth walking all those miles for! Wasn't he funny?

Now one day Pinny, one of his friends, thought he would have a joke with Roundabout. He was walking out with him in the woods, and suddenly Pinny saw a big bird, a black and white magpie, sitting on a tree nearby.

"Roundabout!" said Pinny solemnly, stopping quite still. "Shall I tell you something?"

"Yes, do," said Roundabout, "especially if it's about something to eat. I feel hungry."

"That's nothing new," said Pinny. "Well, now listen—there's a pie up in that tree. Look!"

Pinny pointed to the tree in which the magpie sat. Roundabout licked his lips and looked up at the tree. He thought that Pinny meant a real pie.

"Is it a meat-pie?" he asked.

"It's a bird-pie," said Pinny, laughing to himself.

"I can't see it," said Roundabout.

"Well, go and look for it," said Pinny.

Roundabout at once went to the tree and began to climb it. He was far too fat for climbing trees and he found it very difficult. But he wouldn't give up if there was a pie anywhere about—no, not he! Up he went, panting and puffing, looking for that pie.

How he looked! He peered down into the trunk. He put his hand into every hole. He parted the leaves and looked carefully where they grew the thickest. But he couldn't find any pie.

He climbed higher up and looked there. The big magpie looked at him, puzzled. What was this fat goblin doing? Was he looking for her nest?

She began to chatter angrily at him. He looked at her in surprise.

"What's the matter?" he asked. "Are you looking for that pie, too?"

"Pie? What pie?" asked the big bird. "There isn't any pie here, I can tell you! This tree is mine."

"Nonsense!" said Roundabout. "You can't take trees for yourself like that. Tell me where that pie is."

"I don't know *where* it is," said the magpie crossly. "I'm sure there isn't one in my tree. I wish you'd go away. What do you want with a pie, anyway?"

"I want to eat it," said Roundabout. "I'm very hungry."

"What's the pie like?" asked the magpie, thinking that perhaps she might have a peck at it too.

"It's a bird-pie," said Roundabout, "and it's in this tree, I know."

No sooner had he said that than the bird remembered that her name was magpie. She at once thought that the goblin was looking for her or for her little ones. She was very angry indeed, and she flew at the surprised goblin.

"So you came to eat *me*, did you?" she cried in a rage. "Take that! Peck-peck-peck! And that! Peck-peck-peck!"

Roundabout nearly fell off the branch in surprise. He held on tightly, and tried to stop the magpie from pecking him, but she was far too cross to stop.

"Peck-peck-peck!" She pecked off his round hat and threw it to the ground. She pecked off his coat and made two big holes in it. She pecked a big piece out of his trousers and pulled off both his shoes.

"Stop, stop!" cried Roundabout in a panic. "I'll climb down at once if you'll stop pecking me. I don't care about any pie. I'll get down, truly I'll get down, and never come here again."

The magpie gave him one more peck for luck, and then let Roundabout get down. He was in such a hurry that he fell down part of the way, and bounced like a rubber ball on the grass.

"Goodness!" he cried. "That's the last time I go after pies."

He found his shoes and his hat. He picked up his coat and looked at the two big holes. He stuffed a large green leaf into his trousers to hide the hole there, and then he looked about for Pinny, his friend. But Pinny had gone back to the village to tell the folk what a joke he had played on Roundabout, sending him up a tree to look for a pie to

eat—when all the time there wasn't a pie at all, but only a magpie.

All the little folk came running out of the village to see the fun—and they met poor Roundabout limping back in rags, looking very sorry for himself.

" Hallo ! " he said, when he saw Pinny. " I didn't find that pie you told me about—and a very nasty bird nearly pecked me to pieces ! "

" Poor Roundabout ! " said Pinny. " That bird was the pie —it was a magpie. I didn't think it would set about you like that."

" Good gracious, was that the pie ? " asked Roundabout, surprised. " Well, no wonder it got angry when I said I wanted to eat it ! That's taught me a lesson. I'll never eat a pie again ! "

Roundabout kept his word for two whole days, and then, I'm sorry to say, someone sent him an apple-pie—and he ate it all up before you could say " Jack Robinson " !

But you've only got to mention Mag-pie to make him shiver all over !

Feefo Goes to Market

ONCE upon a time there was a gnome called Feefo who made a lot of money out of onion puddings. He grew specially big onions in his garden, and when they were ready he made them into such delicious puddings that you could smell them for miles.

Feefo had a wife and nine children, so although he made a lot of money he never grew rich, because there was always so much to buy for his children.

One day he sold sixteen onion puddings and made so much money that he really thought he would go and have a Big Spend. So he called his wife and asked her what he should spend his money on.

"You shall each have something," he said, rattling his money. "Tell me what you would like."

"Buy me two nice big frying-pans," said his wife, beaming all over her face. "I'd like those very much. And buy nine tin buckets and nine tin spades for the children to dig with. They are always asking for those."

"Very well," said Feefo. "I will go to the town next market-day and buy all those things for you and the children. And for myself I will buy a red waste-paper basket. I have always wanted one."

Mrs. Feefo was so delighted to think she had such a generous husband that when she had finished her washing that day she popped in next-door to her neighbour, Mother Apple, and told her all about it.

"Feefo is buying me two new frying-pans next market-day," she said proudly. "And he is getting the nine children

a tin spade and a bucket each.
What do you think of that?"

Mother Apple thought a lot
about it, but she didn't say
much to Mrs. Feefo. She kept it
all for Father Apple when he
came home that night.

"Why can't you be generous
like Mr. Feefo, the gnome?" she
cried. "He is getting his nine
children a tin spade and bucket
each, and two frying-pans for
his wife. You never buy *your*
family anything like that!"

Mother Apple told Dame
Tickles about it, and Dame
Tickles wished that Mr. Tickles
was as generous as the gnome
Feefo. She told him so when he came home, and he grew
quite cross. She told Mrs. Twiddle about it too, and Mrs.
Twiddle told her neighbour, Mother Bun, how generous the
gnome Feefo was to his wife and children; and they all of
them scolded their husbands because they didn't go to the
market and buy frying-pans and tin buckets and spades.

Now Father Apple, Mr. Tickles, Mr. Twiddle and Father
Bun felt very cross with Feefo for being so generous.

"What does he want to go buying things like that for?"
they said to one another. "It only makes our wives and
children think we are mean because we don't do the same.
We ought to do something about it."

Poor Apple, Twiddle, Tickles and Bun! Wherever they
went they heard about the gnome Feefo going to market on
Saturday to get frying-pans and spades and buckets. And at
last they put their heads together and thought of a plan.

" We will lie in wait for him at the bottom of Breezy Hill," they said. " We will jump out at him and take away all the things he has bought, and then he will not be able to go home and give presents to his wife and children."

So on Saturday they set off to Breezy Hill, after seeing Feefo the gnome walking gaily off to market, jingling his money in his pocket.

" It is hot," said Father Bun. " Let's go and sit on the top of the hill where there is a breeze. We shall easily see Feefo coming and can get down to the bottom long before he is at the top."

So up the hill they went and sat down in a ring on the top. Twiddle smoked his pipe, Bun chewed a grass, and the other two just sat and did nothing, feeling rather sleepy. Soon Twiddle pointed away in the distance, and said that he could see Feefo coming home from market.

Down the hill they went and hid in the bracken at the bottom, meaning to jump out at the gnome when he came walking by.

Feefo had a lot to carry. He had the two frying-pans, and nice big ones they were, too —he had nine tin buckets and nine tin spades—and a fine red waste-paper basket for himself. They were all very awkward to carry and when he reached the top of Breezy Hill he stopped to have a rest.

He sat down and mopped his head. Then he suddenly caught sight of a small yellow button lying not far off. He picked it up.

"Father Bun has been here," he said to himself. "He's been sitting down over there. Dear me, the grass is very flattened just there. He must have had some others with him."

He poked about and found a red match, which he looked at very closely.

"Now who uses red matches?" he thought. "Let me see—yes, Mr. Twiddle does. He's been here too, and not so long ago, either. And here's a handkerchief left behind. It's got a name on it—Tickles. Ho, so *he's* been here too. That means that Apple was here as well, because they do everything together. Now why should Twiddle, Apple, Tickles and Bun all come up here on this hill today and sit here together?"

He sat down and thought. Then he got up and looked on every side of the hill, shading his eyes with his hand.

"They're nowhere to be seen," he said. "That's funny. Are they hiding somewhere? And if they *are* hiding, why should they do such a funny thing?"

Then Feefo suddenly guessed that Twiddle, Tickles, Apple and Bun were keeping a look-out for him, and meant to jump on him and take away the things he had bought. And he sat down and grinned to himself. He would go down the hill all right—but he didn't think they would jump on him. Ho, ho!

Feefo got some string out of his pocket and tied the tin spades in a row together. He slung them over his left shoulder. Then he strung the handles of the tin buckets together and slung these over his right shoulder. Then he put the red waste-paper basket firmly on his head and took the frying-pans up, one in each hand. How strange he looked!

"Now here we go!" he said to himself with a big grin on his cheeky face. He began to run down the hill, and as he ran he shouted at the top of his voice.

"Ho, ho, ho! Make way for Hanky-Panky, the Snorting

Bing-Bong with his clinking, clanking, clonking Fire-eaters! Ho, ho, ho, here I come, Hanky-Panky, snorting and snuffling, the great and dangerous Bing-Bong!"

As he ran and bounded in the air, all the nine tin buckets clanged together and all the tin spades crashed on one another, making a simply fearful din. The red waste-paper basket jumped up and down as Feefo leapt in the air, and all the time he banged his two frying-pans together with a terrible crashing noise.

Goodness, what a fearful sight he looked, and what an awful noise he made! How the spades crashed and smashed together, how the buckets clanked and clinked, and as for the two frying-pans they sounded so terrifying that everyone thought the end of the world had come!

"Ho, ho, ho! Make way for Hanky-Panky, the Snorting Bing-Bong with his clinking, clanking, clonking Fire-eaters! Ho, ho, ho! here I come, Hanky-Panky, snorting and snuffling, the great and dangerous BING-BONG!"

When Twiddle, Bun, Tickles and Apple heard this terrible

noise and saw this awful creature tearing down the hill with a great red hat on his head, banging and clanking, with long strings of things crashing behind him, they fell over one another with fright.

"Get out of his way, quick ! Get out of his way !" they cried to one another, and they fell over each other's legs in their hurry. Poor Twiddle had fallen asleep whilst he was waiting, and he awoke to see the terrifying creature racing down the hill not far from him. He was so frightened that his legs bent under him when he tried to run, and he fell, bumping his nose on the ground.

Feefo the gnome was enjoying himself very much. On and on he ran, shouting and jumping high into the air, all the tin buckets and spades flying out behind him, making more noise than ever, banging the two frying-pans in front of him, trying not to laugh at the sight of the four scrambling gnomes

in front of him, struggling their hardest to get out of his way.

He passed them at a run, leaping his highest, whilst they dived into the bracken and hid, trembling and shaking. Then, when he had left them well behind him, Feefo sank down on the ground and began to laugh. The tears came into his eyes and ran down his long nose to the ground, where they made a big puddle.

How he laughed! He rolled on the ground and roared till his sides ached. Then he sat up and wiped his eyes.

"Dear, dear me," he said. "What a joke that was! I shall never laugh so much again. Ho, ho! Make way for Hanky-Panky, the Snorting Bing-Bong!"

He got to his feet, took the basket off his head and went peacefully home. He gave his wife and children their presents and they were delighted. Then he lighted his pipe and went to lean over his front gate, waiting for Twiddle, Bun, Tickles and Apple to come home.

At last they came, looking white and scared, turning round to look behind them every now and again.

"Hallo!" called Feefo. "What's the matter?"

"Oh, Feefo, didn't you see the Snorting Bing-Bong with his clinking, clanking, clonking Fire-eaters?" cried Twiddle. "He came tearing down Breezy Hill not so long ago."

"Yes, it was Hanky-Panky, snorting and snuffling, the great and dangerous Bing-Bong," said Bun, trembling. "He trod on my toe when he passed and it has swelled up to twice its size."

"He's a fearful person," said Apple. "Didn't you see him, Feefo? He's twice as big as you are, and wears an enormous red hat."

"Oh, yes, I know Bing-Bong," said Feefo. "He's a great friend of mine. I know him as well as I know myself, and I'm very fond of him. I know why he came, too."

c

" Why ? " asked Twiddle, in surprise.

" He came because he knew that there were enemies waiting for me round the corner," said Feefo solemnly. " He came to eat them up. Fancy that ! No wonder you were frightened when you met him."

Twiddle, Tickles, Bun and Apple looked very guilty, indeed. Could it really be that the Bing-Bong had known of their plan to jump on Feefo that afternoon ? Ooh, what an escape they had had !

" Where is he now ? " asked Apple fearfully.

" He's here," said Feefo. " Would you like to see him ? "

" OOOOOOOOOOH ! " shouted Twiddle, Bun, Apple and Tickles in a great fright, and they took to their heels and ran away as fast as ever they could. And that rascally Feefo ran indoors and banged his two frying-pans together to make them go faster !

Well, well ! He hasn't a single enemy now, and I'm sure I don't wonder at it !

Adventures of the Sailor Doll

ONCE there was a sailor doll, and he lived in Janet's nursery. She was very fond of him, and he went everywhere with her. He was such a smart doll, with a blue velvet uniform and a nice sailor collar and round hat. He had a pink, smiling face, and was the most cheerful person you can imagine !

And then one day a dreadful thing happened to him. A puppy came into the garden where Janet was playing, and began to romp about. Janet was frightened and fled indoors. She left her sailor doll behind her on the grass ! Oh, dear, what a pity !

The puppy saw the doll smiling up at him, and he picked it up in his teeth. He threw the doll into the air. The sailor stopped smiling, for he was frightened.

The doll came down on the grass. The puppy picked him up again and began to nibble him. He nibbled his hat and made a hole. He nibbled his sailor collar and tore it. He nibbled a shoe and got it off.

And then he did a really *dreadful* thing. He chewed one of the sailor's arms off ! He bit it right off, and there it lay on the grass beside the poor scared doll.

Then there came a whistling, and the puppy's master came along. The puppy heard the whistling, ran to the gate, and darted out to his master. Off he went down the road, galloping along, leaving behind him the poor chewed sailor.

Well, Janet's mother very soon came out to clear up her little girl's toys, and she saw the sailor doll lying on the grass with his arm beside him. She was very sorry. She picked him up and looked at him.

"I'm afraid you're no more use," she said. "You'll have to go into the dust-bin, sailor. You are all chewed, and you have lost an arm."

She put him on the seat and went on collecting the other toys. The sailor doll was so horrified at hearing he would have to go into the dust-bin that he lay and shivered. Then, seeing that Janet's mother was not looking, he quietly picked up his chewed arm, put it into his pocket, jumped down from the seat, and slipped away into the bushes. *He* wasn't going to be put into the dust-bin! Not he!

Janet's mother was surprised to find he had gone; but it was getting dark, so she went in with the other toys and didn't bother any more about the sailor. As soon as she had gone the sailor slipped out of the bushes and ran down the garden path. He went into the field at the end of the garden and walked over the grass.

He didn't know where he was going. He was just running away from the dust-bin. He went on and on, and soon the moon came up and lighted everything clearly. Still he walked on. He met a hedgehog ambling along looking for beetles,

and a mole with a long snout, and heard two mice quarrelling in the hedges. Still he went on—and at last he could go no further. He was really quite tired out. He had come to a little stream, and being a sailor doll he loved the sound of water.

"I think I'll settle down here for the night," thought the sailor. "I can go on in the morning. I think I am far enough away from that dust-bin now."

So he crept under a dock leaf and lay down. Soon the moon went behind a great cloud, and it began to rain. A goblin crept under the dock leaf to shelter and, finding the sailor there, pushed him away. So the rain poured down on the poor sailor doll and soaked him through. He was so tired he didn't wake up till the morning—and then what a shock he had!

His sailor suit had shrunk in the rain and was now far too

small for him. His hat had shrunk too, and looked very silly perched right on top of his head. His trouser legs were up to his knees, and his coat would no longer meet. He really looked dreadful.

He walked out into the sunshine, and how he sneezed, for he had caught a cold in the rain :

" A-tishoo ! A-tishoo ! "

" Hallo, hallo ! " said a small voice, and the sailor doll saw an elf peeping at him. " What's the matter with *you* ? You look a bit of a scarecrow ! What are you ? "

" I am supposed to be a sailor doll," said the sailor humbly. " I know I look dreadful now."

" Well, you've got a bad cold," said the elf. " Come into this rabbit-hole and I'll make a fire and dry you."

The doll followed the elf, and to his enormous surprise he saw that down the rabbit-hole was a small door, neatly fitted into the side of the burrow. The elf opened the door, and inside was a cosy room with a fire laid ready for lighting. Soon it was crackling away cheerfully. The doll dried his clothes and felt more cheerful, especially when the elf brought him some hot lemonade and some ginger biscuits. Aha ! This was good !

" Now you must get on to my sofa and have a good rest," said the elf kindly. " You can stay here all day in the warmth, if you like."

So he did ; and when the night came, the elf said he might sleep there too.

" I am going to a boating party," she said. " It's being held on the stream. So you can sleep here all night, if you like. I shan't be back till dawn."

" A boating party ! " said the sailor doll, excited. " Oh, can't I come ? "

" No, it would be better for you to stay here in the warm and get rid of your cold," said the elf.

She put on a cape and ran out. The doll wished he knew what a boating party was like. He had never been to one. He opened the door and went into the rabbit-hole to see if he could hear any merry shouts and screams from the boating party. At first he heard laughter and shouts—and then he heard a great crying :

" Oh ! Oh ! You horrid frogs ! Go away ! You are spoiling our party ! "

Then there came a sound of splashing and screaming. Whatever could be happening ?

The doll ran out into the moonlight—and he saw a strange sight. The elves had many little silver boats on the stream, and a great crowd of green frogs had popped up to sink the little boats.

One after another they were pulled under by the mischievous frogs. The elves flew out of the boats as soon as they began to sink, but they were most unhappy because they had lost their pretty boats, and the party was spoilt.

The sailor doll ran to the bank in anger. " How dare you do such a thing, frogs ? " he cried. " I will go and tell the ducks to come here and eat you ! "

The frogs swam off in fright. But not a single boat was left !

" A-tishoo ! " said the sailor doll. " I *am* sorry I didn't come before ! "

" Our party is spoilt ! " wept the little elves. " We have no more boats—and oh, we were having *such* fun ! "

A bright idea came into the sailor doll's head.

" I say," he said, " I know how to make boats out of paper. They float very well too. I used to watch Janet making them. If you can get me some paper, I could tell you how to make them."

The elves gave a shout of delight and ran off. Soon they came back with all sorts of pieces of paper, and they placed them in front of the doll.

"I wish I could make the boats for you," he said, "but, you see, I have only one arm, so I can't. But I will tell you how to do it. Now—fold your paper in half to begin with."

The elves all did as he said, and soon there were dozens of dear little paper boats all ready to float on the river. Lovely!

The elves launched them, and presently another boating party was going on. The frogs didn't dare to appear this time, so everything went off merrily.

In the middle of the party a big ship with silver sails came floating down the stream.

"Look! Look! The Fairy King and Queen are sailing to-night, too!" shouted the elves in glee.

"Let us float round them in our paper boats and give them a hearty cheer!"

So they did; and the King and Queen were *most* astonished

to see such a fleet of boats appearing round their ship, full of cheering elves.

"Go to the bank and anchor there," the King commanded. So the ship was headed for the bank and very soon it was anchored there, and the elves went on board to bow and curtsy to their majesties.

"Who has taught you how to make these lovely boats?" asked the Queen, in surprise. "I have never seen any like them before!"

"The sailor doll did," said the little elf who had helped the doll. She told the King all about the boating party spoilt by the frogs, and how the doll had taught them to make paper boats.

"Bring him here!" commanded the King. But the sailor doll was shy and didn't want to go before their majesties.

"I am all dirty and wet, and my suit is too small for me," he said. "Besides, I have lost an arm, and I am ashamed of having only one. Also, I have a bad cold, and I should not like to give it to the King or Queen. A-tishoo!"

So the elf told the King what the doll had said, and the King nodded his head.

"See that the doll is given a new suit," he said, "and do what you can about his arm, elf. Then send him to me at the palace. I want to speak to him about something very important."

The elf took the surprised sailor doll back to her cosy home in the burrow. She looked him up and down and pursed up her tiny mouth.

"You'll have to have a new suit altogether," she said. "It wouldn't be any good patching up the one you have on. I can get you a new hat made too. The only thing that worries me is your arm. I don't know how I can get you one to match your own."

"Oh, I've got my old one in my pocket," said the sailor doll, and he pulled out his chewed arm.

"Oh, splendid!" said the elf. "Now look here, sailor, just take off all your old clothes, whilst I go to fetch little Stitchaway the Pixie to measure you for a new suit. You can put on my dressing-gown. Sit by the fire and drink some more hot lemon. Your cold seems better already."

She went out. The doll took off his old, dirty suit, put on the elf's little dressing-gown, and sat down by the fire. He was very happy. Things seemed to be turning out all right, after all.

Soon the elf came back with a small pixie who was all hung about with pin-cushions, scissors, and needle-books. With her she carried a great bunch of bluebells.

"Good-day, sailor," she said. "I shall have to make your suit of bluebells. I hope you won't mind, but that is the only blue I have at the moment. Now, stand up, and let me measure you."

It didn't take long to measure the sailor. No sooner was this done than two more pixies appeared. One was a shoemaker, and he soon fitted a pair of fine black boots on the sailor and took away his old ones. Then the other pixie, who was a hatter, and wore about twenty different hats piled on his head, tried them all on the sailor, and found a little round one that fitted him exactly. It had a blue feather in it, but the elf said that it looked very nice, so the sailor left it in.

"Now where's your arm?" said the elf. The doll took his arm from the shelf where he had put it whilst he was being measured. The elf fitted it neatly into his shoulder, said a few magic words, and let go. The arm was as good as ever! The doll could use it just as well as he could use the other one. He was so delighted!

In two days' time the dressmaker elf came back with the grandest blue sailor suit of bluebells that you can imagine! When the sailor dressed himself in it, he did feel smart. The elf looked at him in admiration.

"You look like the captain of a ship," she said. "Now come along to the palace, and we'll see what the King wants."

Well, what *do* you suppose His Majesty wanted? The captain of his fairy fleet was old, and was going to leave the sea and live in a little cottage with his wife. The King wanted another captain—and that was why he had sent for the sailor doll.

"Will you be my new captain?" he asked him. "You look so cheerful, always smiling—and the way you sent off those wicked frogs, and taught the elves how to make new boats, was wonderful. I'd very much like you to be my new captain."

"Oh, Your Majesty, it's too good to be true!" cried the doll, blushing all over his smiling face. "I promise you I will do my very best."

"Very well. You are my captain, then!" said the King. "Now come and have tea with the Queen and our children. They are all longing to know how to make paper boats."

And now the sailor doll is very important indeed, and everyone in Fairyland salutes him when he goes by. You should see him commanding his ship too! You would never think he was once a poor chewed doll who was nearly put in a dust-bin!

Clickety-Clack

THERE was once a gnome called Clickety-Clack, though nobody knew why. He lived at the top of a very long field in a nice little toadstool house. He was so vain that nobody liked him at all, not even Kindheart the fairy, who liked almost everyone.

Clickety-Clack boasted terribly. He said he could do anything, and most people believed him. He said he was cleverer than witches or wizards, and he didn't think there was anyone in the world who was so powerful as he was.

One day quite a lot of people were outside Clickety-Clack's house. He sold fresh honey, and they had come to buy some and to have a chat with one another. Clickety-Clack was pleased to see so many pennies ready for honey, and he began to boast, as usual.

"I shall be richer than anybody in the kingdom soon," he said. "I've got heaps of gold hidden away."

"It's better to be good than rich," said Kindheart.

"It's better to be healthy than wealthy!" said Twiddles the brownie. "You don't look at all well, Clickety-Clack. You're a thin, skinny creature, you are! I'd be sorry to be you, for all you think yourself so clever and strong!"

Clickety-Clack felt very angry.

"I'm thin because I wish to be thin!" he said. "If I wanted to be fat, like you, Twiddles, I could make myself plump to-morrow!"

"Ooh, story-teller!" said Chipperdee the squirrel. "Nobody can do that!"

"*I* can do anything!" said Clickety-Clack. "I can tell you anything, too!"

"All right, then, tell us what those big birds are that have been flying about high up in the air lately," said Dimity the elf.

"No, make one come down, and we'll all see it," said Twiddles. "Look, there's one ever so high up."

He pointed up into the sky. What he saw was an aeroplane, but he didn't know it. He thought it was some strange bird that groaned as it flew.

Clickety-Clack was fairly caught! How could he do such a thing as make that queer bird come down? Why, he didn't even know enough magic to make a cloud come down, and that was a thing that the youngest fairy knew.

There was nothing for it but to be bold and pretend he could make the bird come down. So he drew a circle round himself, clapped his hands three times, jumped head-over-heels twice and then bawled out a long string of words that didn't mean anything at all.

And just at that very moment the airman decided to land! He saw the long field stretching out below, and as he was running out of petrol, he decided to come down.

He began to go round and round in circles, getting lower each time. The little group below watched the aeroplane in amazement. What a strange bird! How big! What a noise it made!

Twiddles began to feel frightened. It seemed as if the great monster was going to come right on top of them. Chipperdee the squirrel trembled, for he had never heard such a fearsome noise in his life.

"It's got two eyes underneath!" cried Kindheart in fright. "Look—they're red, white and blue! Ooh, tell the nasty thing to go back into the sky, Clickety-Clack!"

"I can't! I can't!" wept Clickety-Clack in terror, his knees shaking beneath him.

"You *can*!" said Twiddles. "You made it come down, so you can make it go up again!"

Down came the aeroplane, lower and lower. It seemed to Clickety-Clack that it was going to knock the chimney off his house. He could bear it no longer. He jumped out of the circle he had made and raced away as fast as his legs could carry him. Down the lane he went, and into the wood. He scuttled down a rabbit-hole and lay at the bottom with his nose in the earth, shaking from head to foot.

"Oh, why did I say I could get it down?" he wailed. "How could I know it would really come? I didn't think it would! Oh, the horrid big bird! It will eat us all up, I'm sure it will!"

All day long Clickety-Clack lay in the rabbit-hole, not daring to move. When night came he ventured out again, and crept back to the long field. He looked up and down —but the strange monster was gone.

"Clickety-Clack!" suddenly cried a voice, making him jump two feet into the air. "Why did you run away? Oh, Clickety-Clack, we *do* think you are clever! We didn't really believe you could

do all the things you said you could—we thought you were boasting—but we know that you can, now !"

Chipperdee the squirrel came leaping down to Clickety-Clack, and soon Twiddles, Dimity and Kindheart came up too.

"That strange monster landed on our field," said Twiddles, "but no sooner did it land than it went up again, and disappeared. Do you know why ?"

Clickety-Clack didn't—but the airman could have told him ; for no sooner did he touch ground than he discovered he had more petrol than he thought, so off he went again. He didn't see Chipperdee the squirrel, Twiddles the brownie, Dimity the elf, or Kindheart the fairy.

They all thought Clickety-Clack was wonderful to have

brought the strange bird down, as he had said he would. They couldn't understand why the gnome didn't boast about it as he generally did. But Clickety-Clack had learnt his lesson. He wasn't going to boast any more, not he! He was going to be very careful indeed what he said or did in the future.

"I'm not going to have any more monsters coming down from the sky!" he thought. "I'll not be vain or conceited any more. People will think much less of me—but that can't be helped."

But the funny thing was that everyone thought much *more* of Clickety-Clack when he became humble and modest. They liked him very much, and often had happy evenings with him in his little toadstool cottage. But as soon as anyone began to talk about the strange bird, Clickety-Clack would get red, and not have a word to say for himself. Nobody could guess why —but I can, can't you?

The Enchanted Bone

THERE was once a greedy tabby cat called Whiskers. He was a dreadful thief, and no one dared to leave anything on the table in case he jumped up and got it. If he found the larder door open, he would slip inside—and then there would be no chicken, no meat, no pie left on the shelves, you may be sure.

Now one day Whiskers went to visit his cousin in Pixieland. His cousin was a wonderfully clever cat, black as soot, with great green eyes and a tail as long as a monkey's. He belonged to a witch and helped her with her spells. He was always pleased to see Whiskers and gave him a saucer of cream.

One day he told Whiskers about a marvellous magic bone that the witch owned.

"Do you know, Whiskers," said the black cat, "that bone is so magic that if you put it on a plate and say:

'Bone, please multiply yourself,
And give me meat to fill my shelf'—

it will at once make more and more and more bones, and you can get the most delicious soup all for nothing!"

Whiskers' eyes nearly fell out of his head with surprise. What a bone! If only he had one like that! He would always be able to have a fine meal then.

"Where does the witch keep that bone?" he asked.

"In the cupboard over there," said the black cat, "but it's always locked."

Whiskers had a good look at the cupboard. Yes, it certainly was locked. There was no doubt about that.

But, do you know, the next time that Whiskers went to visit his cousin, that cupboard door was open! Yes, it really was! And what was more, both the witch and her black cat were away!

"Well, well, well!" said Whiskers in delight. "Here's a chance for me. I'll borrow that bone this morning and make myself a fine collection of bones out of it, and then bring it back again before the witch and my cousin come back."

He slipped into the cupboard. He jumped up on to the shelf. He saw the magic bone there, and taking it in his mouth he jumped down. Then out of the kitchen he went at top speed, the big enchanted bone in his mouth.

He ran home. He took the bone into the back garden and set it down on an old enamel plate, belonging to Spot the dog. And then Whiskers said the magic spell:

"Bone, please multiply yourself,
And give me meat to fill my shelf!"

The bone began to work. My goodness, you should have seen it! It was really marvellous. A big bone grew out of

one end and fell on to the plate. A joint of meat grew out of
the other end and fell right *off* the plate. Whiskers stared in
the greatest surprise and delight. What a feast he would
have! Oh, what a feast!

The bone went on throwing out more bones and more
joints. Soon the back garden smelt of meat, and Spot the dog
woke up in surprise. He sat up. Meat! Bones! Where
could they be? He raced over to Whiskers and stared at the
meat and the bones in astonishment. Then he pounced on a
bone.

"It's mine! It's mine! Drop it, Spot!" hissed Whiskers.
But Spot wouldn't. He crunched up the bone and then started
on a joint of meat.

The next-door dog sniffed the meat and came running in at
the gate. The two dogs next door but one smelt it too and
tore in, yelping happily. Whiskers didn't like strange dogs.
He hissed and spat. But they took no notice of him and
began to eat all the meat and bones.

That was too much for Whiskers. He wasn't going to have
all his magic wasted like that. He caught up the enchanted
bone and ran off with it. But it wouldn't stop growing bones
and meat, and soon half the dogs in the town were after
Whiskers in delight.

Whiskers was frightened almost out of his life. He took
one look round at the dogs and fled on and on. He didn't
dare to drop the magic bone, for he knew it would be eaten
if he did—and then what would the witch say?

He ran right round the town and back again. He came to
his own house once more. The door was open. Whiskers
ran inside and jumped up on to the table.

"Get down, Whiskers, get down!" shouted the cook,
and she stared in astonishment—for into her kitchen poured
dozens of dogs—black dogs, white dogs, brown dogs, spotted
dogs, little ones and big ones, nice ones and nasty ones!

"Shoo! Shoo!" cried the cook, taking up a broom and
hitting the dogs. But they jumped over the broom and leapt
on to the table after Whiskers and the magic bone. Whiskers
mewed in fright and jumped up on to the top shelf of the
dresser. The dogs jumped too—and crash, smash, crash,
smash, down went cups and saucers, dishes and plates. The
cook yelled in rage and smacked dogs right and left with the
broom—but more and more came in!

Then the cook saw that there was only one way of getting
rid of them. She picked up the bones and meat that seemed
everywhere—on the floor and the table and the dresser—
and threw them out into the street as fast as she could. Out
went all the dogs after them! Soon the kitchen was empty
and the cook slammed the door. She glared at Whiskers and
took up her broom again.

"What do you mean by stealing all that meat and bringing

it home?" she said. "Take that, you bad cat—and that!"

Thwack, smack! Poor Whiskers got a dreadful spanking. He squealed and leapt out of the window, still with the magic bone in his mouth. He tore off with it to the witch's house— no dogs following this time because they were all busy in the street, gobbling up the meat and the bones that the cook had thrown out for them.

The witch was at home. So was the black cat. And how they glared at Whiskers when he came in with the stolen bone. The witch took hold of him and gave him a good whipping. As for the black cat, he flew at Whiskers and scratched him down the nose.

"Never come here again," he mewed. "You deserve to be well punished."

"I have been punished," mewed poor Whiskers. "I shall never steal again—not even the hind leg of a kipper!"

He never did—and as for bones, he wouldn't go near them, no matter how nice they smelt! Poor old Whiskers!

Fiddle-de-dee, the Foolish Brownie

FIDDLE-DE-DEE was a young brownie. He lived with his mother in Pudding Cottage, and was very lazy indeed. He simply wouldn't do a thing, though his mother had far more than she could do.

"Now look here, Fiddle-de-dee," she said one day. "You really must help me. Your aunt and uncle are coming to tea, and I want some nice fresh muffins. You must go to the baker's and buy twelve."

So Fiddle-de-dee set off. He bought twelve muffins at the baker's and then started off home. On the way back he felt tired, so he jumped into a 'bus. At the next stop so many people got in that some had to stand.

"May I sit on your knee?" another brownie asked Fiddle-de-dee.

"Certainly," said Fiddle-de-dee—but he had the bag of muffins on his knee, and he wondered what to do with them. He slipped them underneath him, and then pulled the brownie down on to his knee. When the end of the ride came, the other brownie thanked him and they both got off the 'bus. The bag of muffins looked very queer.

How cross Fiddle-de-dee's mother was when she saw them!

"You stupid, silly fellow!" she cried. "You've been sitting on them!"

"Well, I had to put them somewhere," said Fiddle-de-dee. "If *I* hadn't sat on them the other brownie would have, for he sat on my knee. And as he was a lot heavier than I am, I thought it would be better if *I* sat on them!"

"You didn't think that you were *both* sitting on them,

then?" asked his mother. "Now, listen, Fiddle-de-dee—the next time I send you out you must think what you're doing. You should have asked the baker to lend you a tray, and then you should have walked home with the muffins on your head like the muffin man."

"I see," said Fiddle-de-dee, and determined to do better next time.

Now two days later his mother thought it would be nice to have some ice-cream, for the day was hot. So she gave Fiddle-de-dee a shilling and told him to fetch some from the ice-cream shop. He set off, and bought a nice lot. It was in a cardboard box.

He had just left the shop when he remembered how he had been scolded about the muffins.

"Mother said I ought to have brought them home on my head," he said. "Well, I forgot to borrow a tray this time, but I'm sure I can balance this box on my head all right."

So he popped the box of ice-cream on his head, and walked home with it. But the sun was tremendously hot that day and beat down on Fiddle-de-dee all the way home. The ice-cream soon melted and began to run out of the corners of the box. It ran down Fiddle-de-dee's hair and trickled down his neck.

"Ooh!" said Fiddle-de-dee in surprise. "I do feel nice

and cold. It isn't such a hot day after all. I'm not nearly so hot now."

The ice-cream went on trickling down his head and neck all the way home. When his mother saw him she gave a cry of dismay.

"Fiddle-de-dee!" she cried. "Whatever are you doing with the ice-cream, carrying it on your head like that in the hot sun! Oh, how foolish you are! It is all melted now, and you are in a terrible mess! You should have wrapped a damp cloth round the box, and covered it with your coat to keep it cool."

"Oh," said Fiddle-de-dee. "Well, how was I to know that? I'll do better next time."

The next day his mother heard that a fine goose was for sale, and she determined to buy it and keep it for Christmas-time.

"I'll fatten it up," she said, "and when Christmas comes it will make us a good Christmas dinner."

So she sent Fiddle-de-dee to get it. He bought it from the farmer, and set off with the goose. But he hadn't gone very far before he remembered how his mother had scolded him about the ice-cream.

"She said I ought to have wrapped it in a damp cloth and carried it home under my coat," he said. "Well, I must try to take the goose home as she said."

Hanging on a near-by clothes-line was a tablecloth belonging to Mother Wimple. Fiddle-de-dee took it down and soaked it in a pond. Then he wrapped the struggling, angry goose in it, and tried to put it under his coat. But the bird was big and strong, and it was all Fiddle-de-dee could do to hold it.

By the time he reached home his coat and shirt were rent and torn by the goose in its struggles to escape. The tablecloth was in rags, and Fiddle-de-dee was all hot and bothered.

"Oh my, oh my!" groaned his mother, when she saw him. "What *have* you been doing with Mother Wimple's lovely

new tablecloth ? And just look at your clothes, Fiddle-de-dee !
They're only fit for the dustbin now ! And the poor goose is
half dead with fright ! "

" I tried to do as you said," said Fiddle-de-dee, " but the
goose didn't like being wrapped up in a damp cloth, Mother."

" You stupid, foolish boy," said his mother. " Can't a goose
walk ? You should have tied a string round its leg and let it
follow behind you ! "

" I see ," said Fiddle-de-dee, and made up his mind to do
better next time.

A week later his mother wanted him to fetch the joint of
meat from the butcher's, so he set off. He took the leg of
mutton from the man, and turned to go home. Then he
remembered how angry his mother had been with him last

time he had gone on an errand for her, and he tried to think how he should take the meat home.

"Mother said last time I ought to have tied a string to the goose's leg and let it follow behind me!" he thought. "Well, this mutton's got a leg, so I'll tie some string to it."

He found a piece of string in his pocket and carefully tied it to the leg of mutton. Then he threw it behind him, and set off home, dragging the meat after him.

He hadn't gone far when half the dogs and cats in the neighbourhood smelt the meat and came running after it. Fiddle-de-dee turned round and saw them all. He became

frightened and started to run. All the dogs and cats ran too !

He tore home, the meat bumping up and down behind him. He raced in through the kitchen door—and all the cats and dogs came too, snarling, growling and fighting over the leg of mutton !

" Oh, good gracious, oh, my goodness ! " cried his mother. " Whatever will you do next ? What made you bring these creatures home with you ? Oh dear, oh dear, look at that meat ! You surely haven't dragged it home on a piece of string ! "

" Well, that's what you told me to do with the goose, Mother," said Fiddle-de-dee.

" Yes, but a leg of mutton isn't a goose ! " cried his mother, in a temper, and she boxed Fiddle-de-dee's ears. Then she picked up a broom, and shooed the dogs and cats away.

" Shoo, shoo, shoo ! " she shouted.   " Shoo, you cats, shoo, you dogs ! "

When all the animals had gone away she turned to scold Fiddle-de-dee—but he wasn't there. He had gone to put himself to bed ! He thought that would be the safest place for him that day, and he was quite right !

The Elephant and the Snail

ONCE upon a time a great elephant went roaming with the herd in the forest. As he went between the trees, pulling down leaves and fruit to eat, a snail fell off a nearby bush, and went rolling to where the elephant stood.

It was a fine snail, with a big, curly shell, brightly coloured in yellow and brown. It rolled underneath the great foot of the elephant. The big beast felt it rolling there, and lifted his foot to see what it was.

When he saw that it was only a small snail, the elephant put down his foot again, meaning to crush the snail—but the tiny creature spoke earnestly to the elephant:

" Don't crush me! Put down your foot to one side and let me crawl away in safety. I have never done you any harm, so have mercy on me, great elephant."

The elephant was not cruel. He moved his enormous foot away and looked at the yellow and brown snail.

" Well, go in peace," he said. " I will not harm you."

" You are a kind creature," said the snail gratefully, moving away. " One day I may be able to save your life for you in return."

The elephant trumpeted loudly with laughter. " How could a creature like you ever do anything for *me*? " he bellowed. " You think too much of yourself, snail! "

The snail said no more, but slid away as fast as he could for fear the elephant should change his mind and step on him. He hid in the bushes until the herd had gone by. All small creatures feared the heavy tread of the elephants.

The weeks went by. Hunters came to the wood—men who wished to capture the elephants and set them to work.

They built a big enclosure of strong fences with a wide entrance.

"Now," they said to one another, "we know where the herd is. We will surround it and drive it gradually to our enclosure. The elephants will all go inside—and then they will find they cannot get out. They will be caught!"

So the next day the hunters went out to surround the herd. But the elephants were very wary and they had moved off, all except three who were separated from the herd. They were caught, for they ran when they heard the hunters coming, and very soon they had lumbered into the big ring of fencing, and were prisoners.

The three elephants trumpeted in rage. They knew they were caught. They tried to rush out of the gateway—but now the big gate had been closed, and there was no way out. The elephants pushed against the fence, but it was too strong to break down, even when the three of them pushed together. A fence like that would need a whole herd to push it down!

The elephants bellowed with anger, but they could do nothing. One of them was the elephant who had let the snail go free, but he had forgotten all about the little creature by now.

But the snail had not forgotten. When it heard the bellowing of the elephants, it crawled from its hiding-place nearby, and glided up to the top of the fence. On the other side stood the elephant the snail knew so well!

"Friend," said the snail. "Why do you roar so loudly?"

"Because I am caught," said the elephant sulkily. "I cannot get away from here."

"Can I help you?" asked the snail.

The elephant laughed. "Of course not!" he said. "What can a snail like you do, I should like to know? Can you break down this fence? Can you open the gate? No—you are a worthless little snail, and can do nothing!"

"Can your friends help you?" asked the snail.

"Yes, if they were here," said the elephant. "But they do not know where I am. If the whole herd were here they could easily knock down this fence. But before they come wandering by this way again I and the other two elephants here will be taken away."

"I think I *can* help you," said the snail. "I know I crawl very slowly, but if you would tell me where to find your friends, I might be able to get to them in time for them to come here and break down the fence for you."

The elephant stared at the yellow and brown snail in surprise. "You are kind, snail," he said. "But you are such a slowcoach that it would take you weeks to crawl to my friends."

"I will try," said the snail. So the elephant told him where he thought the rest of the herd would be, and the little snail crawled down the fence again and made his way through the forest grass.

Certainly the snail was a slowcoach, but he did not rest for a moment. He kept a sharp look-out for birds, and went on his way steadily. He glided along all night, leaving a silvery trail behind him. He slid along all day, and all the next night too. He was very tired by the middle of the second day; but to his delight he thought he heard the sound of elephants' feet thudding along not far off. He crawled up a tree and waited. Perhaps the herd was coming that way.

It was! As the leader passed the tree on which the snail hung, the little creature called to him:

"Great elephant! I have a message for you."

"Tell me," said the elephant.

"Three of your friends are caught in a big ring of fences," said the snail. "They cannot break the fence down. But if you take the whole herd there, you can break it down between you."

The leader of the elephants spoke to the herd, and they listened, their eyes wise and bright.

"We will come where you lead," they said.

"Snail, crawl on to my head, so that you can tell me the way," said the leader of the elephants. He pressed close to the tree, and the snail dropped to his head. He clung there, and the elephant moved off.

"Who would have thought that I would ride on an elephant at the head of a herd?" thought the little snail, astonished. He told the elephant the way to go, and to his surprise they arrived near the fencing before nightfall.

"When it is dark," said the leader, "we will all go to one part of the fence. We will run against it with all our might and break it down. Keep close by me, and when I trumpet once, charge with me. Snail, crawl down from my head, for you may get hurt. You have been a good friend to us to-day."

The snail crawled down and glided to a thick bush. It waited there in excitement. Before long there came the sound of a trumpeting noise—and the herd of elephants charged together at the great fence.

It went down as if it were made of cardboard. The herd turned and fled, and with them went the three elephants who had been captured, overjoyed at being free again.

The hunters were astonished. "Now, who could have told the herd about the captured elephants?" they cried. "How did the herd know where they were?"

"I could answer your questions," thought the yellow and brown snail. "But I won't! It is good to help a friend!"

The elephant was grateful to the little snail. "I am sorry I laughed at you," he said. "I did not guess, when I gave you your life, that a little thing like you could help *me*."

"Little things are very useful sometimes," said the snail as he glided away.

The Invisible Gnome

THERE was once a gnome called Too-Much. He was called Too-Much because he was very fat, so there was too much of him. He was very greedy, very sly, and not at all to be trusted.

Now one day he stole a hat belonging to a witch. When he put it on—hey presto, he couldn't be seen! Marvellous! The hat was rather small, but that didn't matter—as soon as he wore it Too-Much disappeared—and then, think of the tricks he could get up to!

"I'll use this hat to get myself as many cakes, pies, and apples as I like," thought Too-Much gleefully. "My word, what a time I'll have!"

He clapped on the hat and went off down the street. Nobody could see him. How he chuckled! He went to Dame Biscuit's cake-shop and looked in at the window.

"Currant buns! Doughnuts with jam! Gingerbread fingers! Oooooh! Here I go!" And into the shop he went. His quick fingers took three currant buns, two doughnuts, and six gingerbread fingers. Then out he went. Dame Biscuit was most amazed when she saw the cakes disappearing, and she cried out in rage. "Hi! Come back, cakes!" She could see them travelling through the air, but she couldn't see who was taking them!

But of course the cakes didn't come back. They soon disappeared down Too-Much's throat. Then he went to the pie-shop, and Mister Crusty saw, to his great surprise, three large pies rise into the air and go out of the door. He took a stick and ran after them—but it wasn't long before they went the same way as the cakes.

"This is fine!" said Too-Much in delight. "What a splendid way of getting what I want! Now for a drink!"

He stopped outside the lemonade-shop and looked into the window. Then in he went and took a glass from the counter. The shopkeeper shouted in fear when he saw the glass dipping itself into the jar of lemonade. It came out full, tilted itself up, and out fell the lemonade—and disappeared entirely!

"Oooh! Magic! Bad magic!" yelled the shopkeeper, and ran out into the street, calling people to come and see. But Too-Much slipped out with him and went towards the market-place.

He didn't want anything more to eat and drink for a while, so he amused himself by taking all the farmers' hats off, one by one, and throwing them into the horse-trough.

What an uproar there was in the market! Soon there was a free fight going on, for each farmer thought another had knocked off his hat.

Suddenly a bell rang, and everyone stood still. On the steps of the Town Hall stood Bron, the chief gnome of the town.

"What's all this?" he roared. "You should be ashamed of yourselves."

Too-Much skipped up the steps unseen, took off the chief gnome's hat, and threw it neatly on to the roof of the Town Hall. Bron gaped in astonishment, and everyone roared with laughter.

"It's an invisible gnome!" cried the farmers. "We shall have to catch him, or he will plague the life out of us."

But how? Ah, that was the question.

Too-Much, still wearing the witch-hat, stole sweets, pears, and apples next. Soon the whole town wanted to catch him—and once they very nearly did. Too-Much trod in a puddle—

and suddenly the marks of wet feet appeared on the pavement, though there seemed to be nobody walking there.

"There he is!" cried everyone, and ran after the trail of wet foot-marks. Too-Much, glancing round, saw the townsfolk after him and ran for his life. He tore into the nearest house, which happened to be Mother Twitchet's, and found himself in her parlour. The townsfolk rushed after him, much to Mother Twitchet's surprise and anger, for she was having a nap.

"Shut all the doors," cried Bron, the chief gnome. "He's in here somewhere."

So all the doors were shut. Then Bron made everyone sit down on the floor whilst he went round the room, his hands stretched out as if he were playing Blind Man's Buff. But Too-Much found it easy to slip away, for he could see Bron all the time.

"What are we to do?" groaned Bron. "Someone else try now!"

So the others tried to find Too-Much, but no one could. By this time it was evening, and Mother Twitchet said they must go and leave her in peace.

"But that sly gnome is somewhere about your parlour," said Bron. "You don't want him here all night, do you, snoozing by your fire?"

"Don't you worry—*I* can find him all right," said Dame Twitchet. "You come here in the morning, Bron, and you'll find I've got him for you. It takes a cleverer gnome than this invisible one to get the better of old Mother Twitchet."

"You boast too much," said Bron crossly. "See you keep your word, or I'll have something to say to you to-morrow."

He held the door a very little open, and all the gnomes slipped out. Bron made sure that the invisible gnome did not slip out too, then he went. The door was locked on the outside, and Mother Twitchet was left alone.

"Are you going to show yourself, or shall I make you?" said Mother Twitchet. Too-Much said nothing, but just grinned to himself. Mother Twitchet went to a drawer and took out a little yellow box full of sneezing powder. It was a favourite snuff of hers, very strong indeed. She first wrapped a handkerchief round her nose so that she would not smell it herself, then she took pinches of the powder between finger and thumb and scattered them all over the room.

Too-Much was hiding behind the sofa. As soon as a pinch of snuff flew there, it tickled his nose terribly. He got out his handkerchief and buried his face in it—but the mischief was done.

"A-tishoo!" he said. "A-tishoo! A-tishoo!"

His head jerked as he sneezed, and off flew his tight witch-hat. Mother Twitchet ran to the sofa as soon as she heard the first sneeze and snatched up the fallen hat. Then she dragged Too-Much out—and, my word, the spanking she gave him ! How he howled ! How he yelled !

She tied him up to her mangle—and there he was next day when Bron peeped in at the door. Oh, clever Mother Twitchet !

Mr. Grumpygroo's Hat

MR. GRUMPYGROO was the crossest old man in the whole of Tweedle village. No one had ever seen him smile, or heard him laugh. He was so mean that he saved all his crumbs and made them into a pudding instead of giving them to the birds.

Of course, as you can guess, no one liked him. No one smiled at old Grumpygroo, or said good morning. They frowned at him, or scowled, for no village likes to have such a crosspatch living in it. Grumpygroo didn't seem to mind. He lived all alone in his tumble-down cottage, and made friends with no one.

But he was very lonely. He often wished the children would smile at him as they smiled at the Balloon woman and Mr. Sooty, the Sweep. But they never did, and old Grumpygroo vowed and declared he wouldn't be the first to smile at anyone, not he !

Every day he went walking through the village with his old green scarf round his neck, and his old top-hat on his head ; and he might have gone on scowling and frowning for ever, if something queer hadn't happened.

One morning he went into the hall to fetch his scarf and his hat. It was rather a dark day, and old Grumpygroo could hardly see. He felt about for his scarf, and tied it round his neck. Then he groped about for his hat.

There was a lamp, unlighted, standing in the hall on the chest where Grumpygroo usually stood his hat. On it was a lamp-shade made of yellow silk with a fringe of coloured beads. By mistake Mr. Grumpygroo took up the shade instead

of his hat. It was so dark that he didn't see the mistake he had made, and he put the lamp-shade on his head! It felt rather like his top-hat, so he didn't notice any difference; and out he walked into the street wearing a bright yellow lamp-shade instead of his old hat.

He looked very funny indeed, for all the beads shook as he walked. Just as he went out of his gate, the clouds fled, the sun came out and all the birds began to sing. It was a perfectly lovely spring day.

Even old Mr. Grumpygroo felt a little bit glad, and he half wished he had a friend who would smile at him. But he knew nobody would, so he set his face into a scowl, and went down the street.

The first person he met was the jolly Balloon woman carrying her load of balloons. As soon as she saw the yellow lamp-shade on Mr. Grumpygroo's head, she smiled, for he looked so very funny.

Grumpygroo thought she was smiling at him, for of course he didn't know what he had on his head, and he was most surprised. He didn't smile back, but went on his way, puzzled to know why the Balloon woman should have looked so friendly for the first time in twenty years.

The next person he met was Mr. Sooty, the village sweep. Mr. Sooty loved a joke, and when he saw the lamp-shade perched on old Grumpygroo's head, he grinned very broadly indeed, and showed all his beautiful white teeth.

Mr. Grumpygroo blinked in surprise. The sweep usually called out something rude after him, and certainly he had never smiled at him before. Could it be the fine spring morning that was making people so friendly?

"I shall smile back at the very next person who smiles at me," said Grumpygroo to himself, feeling quite excited. "If people are going to be friendly, I don't mind being nice too."

Round the corner he met Straws the farmer riding on his old horse. As soon as the farmer caught sight of the lamp-shade, he smiled so widely that his mouth almost reached his ears.

And Grumpygroo smiled back! Straws nearly fell off his horse with astonishment, for no one had ever seen such a thing before! He ambled on, lost in surprise, and Grumpygroo went on his way with a funny warm feeling round his heart.

"I've smiled again!" he said to himself. "I've forgotten how nice it was. I hope someone else smiles at me, for I wouldn't mind doing it a second time."

Four little children came running up the street. As soon as they saw Grumpygroo with the yellow lamp-shade on his head, they smiled and laughed in delight.

Grumpygroo was so pleased. He smiled too, and the ice round his heart melted a little bit more. The children laughed merrily and one of them put her hand in his, for she thought Grumpygroo had put the lamp-shade on to amuse her.

Something funny happened inside Grumpygroo. He wanted to sing and dance. He wanted to give pennies away and hug someone. It was lovely to have people so friendly towards him. He put his hand in his pocket, and brought out four bright pennies. He gave one to each child, and they kissed him and ran to the sweet-shop to spend their money, waving and laughing as they went.

Mr. Grumpygroo rubbed his hands in delight. It was lovely to be smiled at and kissed. He would show the people of Tweedle village what a fine, generous person he was, now that they were being so nice to him!

The next person he met was Mr. Crumbs, the baker. Grumpygroo smiled at him before Mr. Crumbs had time to smile first. The baker was so surprised that he nearly dropped the load of new-made cakes he was carrying. Then he saw Grumpygroo's lamp-shade hat, and he gave a deep chuckle. Grumpygroo was delighted to see him so friendly.

"Good morning," he said to Crumbs. "It's a wonderful day, isn't it?"

The baker nodded his head and laughed again.

"Yes," he said; "and that's a wonderful hat you're wearing, Mr. Grumpygroo."

Grumpygroo went on, very much pleased.

" What a nice fellow to admire my old top-hat," he thought. " Dear, dear me, and I always thought the people of Tweedle village were so unpleasant. That just shows how mistaken I can be ! "

He smiled at everyone he met, and everyone smiled back, wondering why Grumpygroo wore such a funny thing on his head. The children loved it, and the old man gave away so many pennies that he had to change a shilling into twelve more, or he wouldn't have had enough.

By the time he reached home again, he was quite a different man. He smiled and hummed a little tune, and he even did a little jig when he got into his front garden. He was so happy to think that people had been friendly to him.

" It shows I can't be so grumpy and cross as they thought I was," he said to himself. " Well, well, I'll show them what a fine man I am. I'll give a grand party, and invite everyone in the village to it. Whatever will they say to that ! "

He walked into his hall, and was just going to take off his hat when he saw himself in the glass. He stood and stared in surprise and dismay—whatever *had* he got on his head !

" Oh my, oh my, it's the lamp-shade ! " he groaned, and he took it off. " Fancy going out in that ! And oh dear ! Everyone smiled at the lamp-shade, because it looked so funny—they didn't smile at *me* ! "

How upset Grumpygroo was ! He sat down in his armchair and thought about it, and after a while he became very much ashamed of himself.

" How dreadful to have to wear a lamp-shade on my head before people will smile at me ! " he groaned. " I must be a most unpleasant old man. Well, well ! I don't see why I shouldn't have my party. Perhaps the village folk will learn to smile at me for myself if I am nice to them. I'll send out those invitations at once ! "

He did—and wasn't everybody surprised !

"Fancy old Grumpygroo giving a party!" they said. "Something must have happened to make him nicer! Do you remember how funny he looked yesterday when he wore that lamp-shade?"

The party was a great success, and soon old Grumpygroo had heaps of friends. Nobody could imagine what had changed the old fellow and made him so nice, nor could anyone understand why he kept his old yellow lamp-shade so carefully, long after it was dirty and torn.

But Grumpygroo knew why! It had brought him smiles and plenty of friends—but he wasn't going to tell anyone that—not he!

The Fairy and the Policeman

ONE night a fairy wandered into the nursery, where the toys were all talking and playing together. They were delighted to see her, and begged her to tell them all about herself.

"Well, I live under the white lilac bush in the garden," she said. "But, you know, I'm afraid I shall soon have to move."

"Why?" asked the toys in surprise.

"Because," said the fairy with a shiver, "a great fat frog has come to live there. I don't mind frogs a bit usually, but this one likes to cuddle close to me, and he *is* so cold and clammy! When I move away from him he gets angry. I am so afraid that he will bring his brothers and sisters there too, and if they all cuddle up to me for warmth I'm sure I shall die!"

"Dear me," said the toy policeman, in a shocked voice. "But, you know, my dear little fairy, frogs have no right to go to the place you have made your home. That is trespassing, and isn't allowed."

"Well, how can I prevent them?" said the fairy. "They are much stronger than I am."

"Look," said the toy policeman, taking a whistle from his pocket. "Here is a police whistle. Take it home with you to the lilac bush. If those frogs do come, blow it loudly and I will come to your help."

"Oh, thank you," said the fairy, and she slipped the whistle into her pocket. Off she went, out of the window, waving merrily to the toys.

And the very next night, just as the toys were playing "Here we go round the Mulberry Bush," they heard the police whistle being blown very loudly indeed.

"The fairy is whistling for help!" cried the policeman, and he jumped out of the window. He ran to the white lilac bush, and underneath he saw such a strange sight.

There were seven yellow and green frogs, all crowding round the poor little fairy, and she was *so* frightened. The policeman drew his truncheon, and began to smack the frogs smartly. Smack! Smack! They squeaked and croaked in pain and began to hop away.

The fairy threw her arms round the brave policeman's neck and hugged him.

"Come back to the nursery with me," begged the toy policeman. "You'll be safe there. I'm afraid the frogs might come back again when you are asleep."

So the fairy went back to the nursery with the policeman, and all the toys welcomed her. She played games with them and had a perfectly lovely time. When they were hungry they went to the little toy sweet-shop and bought some peppermint rock. It was great fun !

" I do wish I could live here with you," said the fairy. " It's so jolly."

" Well, why can't you ? " asked the policeman. " There's plenty of room in the toy cupboard. We can hide you right at the back."

So that night the fairy slept in the toy cupboard with all the other toys—and what do you think ? Early the next morning Gwen, the little girl who lived in the nursery, went to the cupboard and began to pull all the toys out. Oh, how the fairy trembled !

" Keep quite still and pretend you are a toy doll," whispered the policeman. So she did.

" Oh, oh ! Here's a beautiful fairy doll ! " cried Gwen,

suddenly seeing the fairy. "Where did she come from? Oh, Mummy, look!"

She pulled out the doll and showed it to her mother. The fairy kept so still and made herself so stiff that she really did look just like a fairy doll.

"Isn't she beautiful?" cried the little girl. "Where did she come from, Mummy?"

"Well, really, I don't know," said Mummy, surprised. "I've never seen her before. It's the nicest toy you have, Gwen."

Gwen played with the fairy doll all day long and loved her very much. The fairy was delighted, and when night came and all the toys came alive once more, she danced round the nursery in joy.

"I shall be a toy now instead of a fairy," she cried. "I shall live with you in the cupboard and be happy."

"Hurrah!" shouted the toys. "What fun!"

The fairy is still there, and Gwen is very fond of her. Wouldn't she be surprised if she knew that her doll is really a fairy?

The Little Red Squirrel

ONCE upon a time Leslie and Gladys went to look for nuts. They hunted in the hazel hedges, but not a single nut could they find. They looked for the bigger hazel trees, but even there they could only find two or three nuts.

"We shall never get our basket full," said Gladys. "I wonder where the best nuts are? The children we saw coming home from nutting last week had hundreds of nuts."

"Well, perhaps that's why we can't find any," said Leslie. "They've picked them all."

"Listen!" said Gladys, stopping. "There are some other children in the woods this morning."

"Let's see if they know any good nut trees," said Leslie. So the two children ran between the trees and came to where three boys were.

And what do you suppose they were doing? You will never guess, because it was so horrid.

They had found a little red squirrel up an oak tree and they were throwing stones at it ! Wasn't it unkind ? The oak tree was standing quite alone with no other trees near it, so that the little squirrel couldn't jump to another tree and escape that way. It did not dare to run down the trunk of the oak tree, for it was afraid it would be hit.

So there it sat up in the tree, looking as frightened as could be ! When Gladys and Leslie saw what was happening they were very angry and upset. They rushed up to the boys and shouted to them :

" Stop! Stop ! You mustn't do that ! That is very cruel ! "

But the boys only laughed. So what do you think Leslie did ? He climbed quickly up the tree, and then said, " Now throw stones if you like ! And if you hit *me* my sister will tell the keeper of the wood, and you will all get into trouble ! "

Well, the boys did not dare to throw stones when Leslie was in the tree, so they stopped, and very soon went away. Leslie slid down the tree. Gladys hugged him.

" That was a brave thing to do, Leslie," she said. " The boys might have gone on throwing stones and hit you hard."

The red squirrel peered down at the two children. It had a dear little face with big black eyes. Its tail was very bushy. It made a little chattering noise and came bounding down the tree to Gladys and Leslie.

" Oh, it's quite tame," said Gladys, pleased. The squirrel bounded to their basket and looked inside. Gladys wondered if it wanted a nut, so she held one of her few nuts out to the little creature. But it did not take it. Instead it ran off between some bushes. Then it stopped and looked back at the children and made a chattering noise again.

" Look ! " said Gladys. " I believe it wants us to follow it, Leslie ! Come on ! "

They ran after the squirrel. It went on again and took them

down a tiny path made by rabbits. The children followed;
and then they suddenly saw what the red squirrel was leading
them to !

He knew where the best nuts were to be found ! He ran
to a group of hazel trees that no one had been to—and dear
me, you should have seen the nuts on their branches ! There
were dozens and dozens—big, ripe, and so pretty in their
green cloaks.

"Oooh !" cried Leslie. "Look ! We can get a basketful
in no time."

And so they did. They pulled the ripe nuts down by the
handful, and soon their basket was overflowing. The children
turned to thank the little red squirrel. It was sitting up in a
nearby tree, watching them out of its big bright eyes, its bushy
tail curled upright behind it.

"Thank you, little red squirrel," cried the children. "It was kind of you to show us where these fine nut trees grew."

The squirrel made a funny little noise that sounded like "Don't mention it!" and bounded off into the trees. The children went home—and on the way whom did they see but the three unkind boys!

"Look!" cried the boys, pointing to Leslie's full basket. "Look. What lovely nuts! Where did you get them from?"

"That's our secret," said Leslie. "The little red squirrel you were teasing took us to some wonderful nut trees. If you had been kind to him he might have shown them to you too. You ought to be ashamed of treating a pretty little creature so cruelly!"

The boys said no more. They ran off—but I expect they wished they had been kind too, don't you?

The Little Walking House

IF it hadn't been for Puppy-Dog Pincher the adventure would never have happened. Jill and Norman were taking him for a walk in Cuckoo Wood, and he was mad with joy. He tore here, there and everywhere, barking and jumping for all he was worth.

The children laughed at him, especially when he tumbled head over heels and rolled over and over on the grass. He was such a fat, roly-poly puppy, and they loved him very much.

Then something happened. Pincher dived under a bramble bush, and came out with something in his mouth. It was a string of small sausages!

"Now wherever could he have got those from?" said Jill, in surprise. She soon knew, for out from under the bush ran a little fellow dressed in red and yellow, with a pointed cap on his head. He wasn't much taller than the puppy, but he had a very big voice.

"You bad dog!" he shouted. "You've stolen the sausages I bought for dinner! Bring them back at once or I'll turn you into a mouse!"

Pincher took no notice. He galloped about with the sausages, enjoying himself very much. Then he sat down to eat them! That was too much for the small man. He rushed at Pincher and struck him on the nose with a tiny silver stick. At the same time he shouted out a string of queer words, so strange that Jill and Norman felt quite frightened. They knew they were magic words, although they had never heard any before.

And then, before their eyes Pincher began to grow small! He grew smaller and smaller and smaller and smaller, and at last he was as tiny as a mouse. In fact, he *was* a mouse, though he didn't know it! He couldn't think what had happened to him. He scampered up to Jill and Norman, barking in a funny little mouse-like squeak.

The children were dreadfully upset. They picked up the tiny mouse and stroked him. Then they looked for the little man to ask him if he would please change Pincher back to a dog again.

But he had gone. Not a sign of him or his sausages was to be seen. Norman crawled under the bramble bush, but there was nothing there but dead leaves.

"Oh, Jill, whatever shall we do?" he said. "We can't take Pincher home like this. Nobody would believe he was Pincher, and he might easily be caught by a cat."

Jill began to cry. She did so love Pincher, and it was dreadful to think he was only a mouse now, not a jolly, romping puppy-dog.

"That must have been a gnome or a brownie," she said, wiping her eyes. "Well, Norman, I'm not going home with Pincher like that. Let's go farther into the wood and see if we meet any more little folk. If there's one here, there must be others. We'll ask them for help if we meet them."

So they went on down the little winding path. Norman carried Pincher in his pocket, for there was plenty of room there for the little dog, now that he was only a mouse.

After they had gone a good way they saw the queerest little house. It had two legs underneath it, and it stood with its back to the children. Norman caught hold of Jill's arm and pointed to it in amazement. They had never seen a house with legs before.

"Oh!" cried Jill, stopping in surprise. "It's got legs!"

The house gave a jump when it heard Jill's voice, and then, oh goodness me, it ran off! Yes, it really did! You should have seen its little legs twinkling as it scurried away between the trees. The children were too astonished to run after the house. They stood and stared.

"This is a funny part of Cuckoo Wood," said Norman. "I say, Jill! Look! There are some more of those houses with legs!"

Jill looked. Sure enough, in a little clearing stood about six more of the queer houses. Each of them had a pair of legs underneath, and shoes on their big feet. They stood about, sometimes moving a step or two, and even stood on one leg now and again, which made the house they belonged to look very lop-sided and queer.

Jill and Norman walked towards the funny houses—but dear me, as soon as they were seen those houses took to their heels and ran off as fast as ever they could ! The children ran after them, but they couldn't run fast enough.

They were just going to give up when they saw one of the houses stop. It went on again, but it limped badly.

"We could catch that one!" said Jill. "Come on, Norman!"

They ran on and in a few minutes they had caught up the limping house. Just as they got near it the door opened and a pixie looked out. She was very lovely, for her curly golden hair was as fine as spider's thread, and her wings shone like dragonfly wings.

"What's the matter, little house?" they heard her say. "Why are you limping?"

Then she saw the children and she stared at them in surprise.

"Oh, so that's why the houses ran off!" she said. "They saw you coming! Could you help me, please, children? I

think my house has a stone in one of its shoes, and I'm not strong enough to get it out all by myself."

Jill and Norman were only too ready to help. Norman held up one side of the house whilst the house put up one of its feet to have its big shoe off. The pixie and Jill found a big stone in the shoe, and after they had shaken it out they put on the shoe again. The little house made a creaking noise that sounded just like "Thank you!"

"What a funny house you've got!" said Jill to the pixie.

" What's funny about it ? " asked the pixie in surprise, shaking back her long curly hair. " It's just the same as all my friends' houses."

" But it's got legs ! " said Norman. " Where we come from, houses don't have legs at all. They just stand square on the ground and never move at all, once they are built."

"They sound silly sort of houses," said the pixie. " Suppose an enemy came ? Why, your house couldn't run away ! Mine's a much better house than yours."

" Oh, much better," agreed Jill. " I only wish I lived in a house like this. It would be lovely. You'd go to sleep at night and wake up in a different place in the morning, because the house might wander miles away."

" I say, pixie, I wonder if you could help us ! " suddenly said Norman. He took the little mouse out of his pocket.

"Look! This was our puppy-dog not long ago and a nasty little man changed him into a mouse. Could you change him back into a dog again ? "

" Oh no," said the pixie. " You want very strong magic for that. I only know one person who's got the right magic for your mouse, and that's High Hat the Giant."

" Where does he live ? " asked Jill eagerly.

" Miles away from here," said the pixie. " You have to go to the Rainbow's End, and then fly up to Cloud-Castle just half-way up the rainbow."

"Goodness, we couldn't possibly go there," said Jill. "We haven't wings like you, Pixie."

"Well, Dumpy the gnome lives near the Rainbow's End," said the pixie. "He keeps pigs that fly, you know, so he might lend you two of them. But I don't know if High-Hat the Giant will help you, even if you go to him. He's a funny-tempered fellow, and if he's in a bad humour he won't do anything for anybody."

"Well, we might try," said Norman. "Which is the way to the Rainbow's End?"

"It depends where there's a rainbow to-day," said the pixie. "I know! I'll get my house to take you there. It always knows the way to anywhere. Come inside and we'll start. You helped me to get the stone out of my house's shoe, and I'd like to help you in return."

The children went inside the house, feeling most excited. Norman had Pincher the mouse safely in his pocket. Pincher kept barking in his squeaky voice, for he couldn't understand how it was that Jill and Norman had grown so big! He didn't know that it was himself that had grown small.

The pixie shut the door, and told the children to sit down. It was a funny house inside, more like a carriage than a house, for a bench ran all round the wall. A table stood in the middle of the room and on it were some dishes and cups. In a corner a kettle boiled on a stove, and a big grandfather clock ticked in another corner.

The clock had two feet underneath it, like the house, and it gave the children quite a fright when it suddenly walked out from its corner, had a look at them and then walked back.

"Don't take any notice of it," said the pixie. "It hasn't any manners, that old clock. Would you like a cup of cocoa and some daffodil biscuits?"

"Oooh yes, please," said both the children at once, wondering whatever daffodil biscuits were. The pixie made a big jug of cocoa and put some funny yellow biscuits on a plate, the shape of a daffodil trumpet. They tasted delicious, and as for the cocoa, it was lovely—not a bit like ordinary cocoa, but more like chocolate and lemonade mixed together. The children did enjoy their funny meal.

Before the pixie made the cocoa she spoke to her house. "Take us to the Rainbow's End," she said. "And be as quick as you can."

To the children's great delight the house began to run. They felt as if they were on the sea, or on the elephant's back at the Zoo, for the house rocked from side to side as it scampered along. Jill looked out of the window. They were soon out of the wood, and came to a town.

"Norman, look! There are hundreds of fairy folk here!" cried Jill, in excitement. So there were—crowds of them, going about shopping, talking and wheeling funny prams with the dearest baby fairies inside. The grandfather clock walked out of its corner to the window too, and trod on Jill's toe. It certainly had no manners, that clock.

They passed right through the town and went up a hill where little blue sheep were grazing. Looking after them was a little girl exactly like Bopeep. The pixie said yes, it really was Bopeep. That was where she lived. It was a most exciting journey, and the children were very sorry when they saw a great rainbow in the distance. They knew they were coming to the end of

their journey in the walking house.

The little house stopped when it came to one end of the rainbow. The children stepped outside. There was the rainbow, glittering marvellously. It was very, very wide, far wider than a road and the colours were almost too bright to look at.

"Now High-Hat the Giant lives halfway up," said the pixie, pointing. "Come along, I'll take you to Dumpy the gnome, and see if he has a couple of pigs to spare you."

She took them to a squat little house not far from the rainbow. Outside was a big yard and in it were a crowd of very clean pigs, bright pink and shining. Each of them had pink wings on his back, so they looked very strange to Jill and Norman.

"Hie, Dumpy, are you at home?" cried the pixie. The door of the house flew open and a fat gnome with twinkling eyes peeped out.

"Yes, I'm at home," he said. "What can I do for you?"

"These children want to fly to High-Hat's," said the pixie. "But they haven't wings. Could you lend them two of your pigs?"

"Yes, if they'll promise to be kind to them," said Dumpy. "The last time I lent out my pigs someone whipped them and all the curl came out of their tails."

"Oh, these children helped me to take a stone out of my house's shoe," said the pixie, "so I know they're kind. You

can trust them. Which pigs can they have, Dumpy?"

"This one and that one," said the fat little gnome, and he drove two plump pigs towards the children. "Catch hold of their tails, children, and jump on. Hold on to their collars, and, whatever you do, speak kindly to them or the curl will come out of their tails."

Jill and Norman caught hold of the curly tails of the two pigs and jumped on. The pigs' backs were rather slippery, but they managed to stay on. Suddenly the fat little animals rose into the air, flapped their pink wings and flew up the shining rainbow. It was such a funny feeling. The pigs talked to one another in queer little squeals, and the children were careful to pat them kindly in case the curl came out of their tails.

In ten minutes they came to a towering castle, set right in the middle of the rainbow. It was wreathed in clouds at the top, and was made of a strange black stone that reflected all the rainbow colours in a very lovely manner. It didn't *seem* a real castle, but it *felt* real enough when the children touched it. They jumped off the pigs' backs and patted them gratefully.

"Stay here, dear little pigs, till we come out again," said Norman. Then he and Jill climbed up the long flight of shining black steps to the door of the castle. There was a big knocker on it shaped like a ship. Norman knocked. The noise went echoing through the sky just like thunder, and quite frightened the two children.

"Come in!" called a deep voice from inside the castle. Norman pushed open the door and went in. He found himself in a great high room full of a pale silvery light that looked like moonlight. Sitting at a table, frowning hard, was a giant.

He was very, very big, so big that Jill wondered if he could possibly stand upright in the high room. He was sucking a pencil and looking crossly at a book in front of him.

"Good morning," said Norman politely.

"It isn't a good morning at all," said the giant snappily. "It's a bad morning.

One of the very worst. I can't get these sums right again."

"Well, bad morning, then," said Jill. "We've come to ask your help."

"I'm not helping anyone to-day," growled the giant. "I tell you I can't get these sums right. Go away."

"We *must* get his help," whispered Norman to Jill. "We'll keep on trying."

"What sums are they?" Jill asked the giant. To her great surprise High-Hat suddenly picked her up in his great hand and set her by him on the table. When she had got over her fright Jill looked at the giant's book.

She nearly laughed out loud when she saw the sums that were puzzling the giant. This was one of them : " If two hens, four dogs and one giant went for a walk together, how many legs would you see? "

"I'll tell you the answer to that," she said. "It's twenty-two ! "

The giant turned to the end of the book and looked. " Yes !" he said in astonishment. " You're right ! But how did you know that? Do another sum, please."

Jill did all the sums. They were very easy indeed. The giant wrote down the answers in enormous figures, and then sucked his pencil whilst Jill thought of the next one.

When they were all finished Norman thought it was time to ask for help again.

"Could you help us now?" he asked. "We've helped *you*, you know."

"I tell you, this is one of my bad mornings," said the giant crossly. "I never help people on a bad morning. Please go away, and shut the door after you."

Jill and Norman stared at him in despair. What a nasty giant he was, after all the help they had given him too ! It really was too bad.

"I don't believe you know any magic at all ! " said Jill. "You're just a fraud ! Why, you couldn't even do easy sums ! "

The giant frowned till the children could scarcely see his big saucer-like blue eyes. Then he jumped up in a rage and hit his head hard against the ceiling. He sat down again.

"For saying a rude thing like that I will punish you!" he growled, in a thunderous voice. "Now listen! You can sit there all the year long and ask me to do one thing after another so that I can show you my power—and the first time you can't think of anything I'll turn you into ladybirds!"

Goodness! Jill and Norman turned quite pale. But in a trice Norman took the little brown mouse out of his pocket and showed it to the giant.

"You couldn't possibly turn this mouse into a puppy-dog, I'm sure!" he cried.

The giant gave a snort and banged his hand on the table. "Homminy, tinkabooroyillabee, juteray, bong!" he cried, and as soon as the magic words were said, hey presto, the little mouse grew bigger and bigger and bigger, and there was Puppy-dog Pincher again, as large as life, and full of joy at being able to run and jump again. But the giant left the children no time to be glad.

"Next thing, please!" he cried.

"Go to the moon and back!" cried Jill suddenly. In a trice High-Hat had vanished completely.

"Quick, he's gone to the moon!" cried Jill. "Come on, Norman, we'll escape before he comes back!"

Out of the castle door they ran, Pincher scampering after them. The two pigs were patiently waiting outside on the rainbow at the bottom of the castle steps. Jill and Norman jumped on their backs, Norman carrying the puppy in his arms. Then quickly the flying pigs rose into the air and flew back to the end of the rainbow.

Just as they got there they heard a tremendous noise far up in the air.

"It's the giant, come back from the moon!" said Jill. "Goodness, what a noise he's making! It sounds like a thunderstorm."

The pixie came running to meet them.

"Is that High-Hat making all that noise?" she asked, looking frightened. "Give the pigs back to Dumpy, and climb into my house again with me. The next thing that happens will be High-Hat sliding down the rainbow after you, and we'd better be gone before he arrives. He'll be in a dreadful temper!"

The pigs were given back to the twinkling gnome, and then the children climbed into the walking house with the pixie and Pincher. Off they went at a great rate, far faster than before. Pincher couldn't understand it. He began to bark and that annoyed the grandfather clock very much. It suddenly came out of its corner and boxed Pincher's ears.

" I'm so sorry," said the pixie. " It's a very bad-mannered clock. I only keep it because it's been in my family for so many years. By the way, where do you want to go to ? "

" Oh, home, please ! " begged the children.

" Right ! " said the pixie. Just as she said that there came the sound of a most tremendous BUMP, and the whole earth shook and shivered.

" There ! That's the giant slid down the rainbow ! " said the pixie. " I knew he would bump himself."

The house went on and on. When it came to a sunshiny stretch of road it skipped as if it were happy.

" Here you are ! " suddenly cried the pixie, opening her door. And sure enough, there they were ! They were in their very own garden at home !

The children jumped out and turned to call Pincher, who was barking in excitement. The grandfather clock suddenly ran out of its corner and smacked him as he went.

" Oh dear, I'm so sorry ! " cried the pixie. " It hasn't any manners at all, I'm afraid. Well, see you another day ! Goodbye, good-bye ! "

The little house ran off, and the children watched it go. What an adventure they had had ! And thank goodness

Pincher wasn't a mouse any longer, but a jolly, jumping puppy-dog!

"Come on, Pincher!" cried Norman. "Come and tell Mother all about your great adventure!"

Off they went and, dear me, Mother *was* surprised to hear their strange and exciting story!

Sly-One's Puzzle

SLY-ONE, the brownie, took up his basket of eggs and butter and set off through the woods to Mother Twinkle's cottage. As he went, he counted the steps he took, for, like you, he sometimes counted things like that, just for fun. When he got to Mother Twinkle's cottage he knocked at the door and gave her the butter.

"It is exactly seven thousand steps from my door to yours," he told her. "Would you think it was so far? It took me eighty minutes to get here."

Then off he went to call on Mister Snips with the eggs. He counted his steps again, just for fun, and to his very great astonishment he found it was exactly seven thousand again, from Mother Twinkle's to Mister Snips's. He looked at his watch and found that it had taken him eighty minutes, as before. Most extraordinary!

Then he turned his steps homeward, and once again he counted them—and what do you think? It was seven thousand steps from Mister Snips's door to Sly-One's own little cottage. "So the distance between each place must be the same," thought Sly-One. "This is very strange. When I go out to tea this afternoon I will tell the others."

So that afternoon Sly-One looked round the tea-table and told his little story—but he thought he would puzzle everyone, so this is how he told it:

"Listen to me. This morning I went to Mother Twinkle's, and I walked seven thousand steps, and it took me eighty minutes. Then I walked from there to Mister Snips's and I took seven thousand steps again in eighty minutes. And then

I walked home, and again I took seven thousand steps—but whatever do you suppose?—I took *an hour and twenty minutes* that time. Why do you think that was?"

"Don't be silly, Sly-One," said Gobo. "If you took the same number of steps you couldn't have taken an hour and twenty minutes. But perhaps you walked more slowly because you were tired."

"No, I wasn't tired," said Sly-One. "I walked just the same pace—really I did."

"Very puzzling!" said Tubby, frowning. "Well, you must have stopped to talk to someone."

"No, I didn't," said Sly-One. "I didn't meet anyone at all. I just went on steadily."

"Now, just think a minute!" said Burly. "Didn't you stop to do up your shoe-lace, or pick up your handkerchief, or gather a few flowers?"

"No," said Sly-One, "I didn't do any of those things."

"Well, you must have made a mistake, then," said Gobo. "It couldn't have taken you *an hour and twenty minutes* to go

exactly the same distance. Your watch must h ave told you wrong."

" My watch keeps perfect time," said Sly-One with a grin. " Do you mean to tell me that not one of you clever brownies can tell me what I want to know ? Really, I didn't think you were so stupid ! "

" It's *you* who are stupid ! " said Gobo. " You can't have taken an hour and twenty minutes that third time. You must. have taken eighty minutes as you did the first two times."

" Well," said Sly-One, " I did ! Eighty minute s *is* an hour and twenty minutes, isn't it ? Ho, ho, ho ! What a joke ! I wonder how many people could see through my puzzle at once ! "

Well, children, did *you* ?

Mr. Widdle on the Train

ONCE a month Mr. Widdle went to see his old mother. He walked to the station, caught the train that went at ten o'clock, spent the day with the old lady, and then came home by the four o'clock train.

And very often when he came home he looked as white as Mrs. Widdle's front doorstep, and could hardly eat any tea at all. Then Mrs. Widdle would shake her head and say: "Really, Mister Widdle, you are no good on a train journey. It does upset you so!"

"I know why it upsets me," said Mister Widdle one day. "I always feel ill when I sit with my *back* to the engine. Now the other day I sat *facing* the engine and I was quite all right. Isn't that strange?"

"But, Widdle dear," said Mrs. Widdle, "if that is all that is wrong with you when you travel, we can soon put that right."

"How?" asked Mr. Widdle in surprise.

"Why, whenever you get into a carriage and find you are sitting with your back to the engine, you must just lean forward to the person in the opposite seat and say: 'Madam (or Sir, if it's a man), I wonder if you will be so kind as to change places with me, as I always feel ill if I sit with my back to the engine.' Then you will change seats and be quite all right."

"Oh, but I couldn't say all that to a stranger," said Mister Widdle, who was a very shy man.

"Oh yes you can if you practise it," said Mrs. Widdle. "Now pretend I am the person opposite, Widdle dear, and say that speech to me."

So Mister Widdle practised saying it till he knew it off by heart. He felt very pleased. Now he would always be able to change places with anyone, and could sit facing the engine and never feel ill. How splendid!

When the day came for him to go to see his old mother, he set off happily, but alas! when he arrived home again that night he looked just as white as ever, and so ill that Mrs. Widdle bundled him into bed at once.

"I *am* disappointed in you, Widdle," she said. "I did think you would say that speech you practised."

"Well, my dear," said Mister Widdle, "it was quite all right when I caught the train at ten o'clock. I got into the carriage and sat down. I began to feel ill because I had my back to the engine, and so I leaned over to the little boy opposite and said: 'I wonder if you'd be so kind as to change

places with me, as I always feel ill if I sit with my back to the engine.' And the nice little chap raised his cap and said: ' Certainly, sir, I don't mind at all.' So we changed places, and I felt as well as could be."

" Well, go on," said Mrs. Widdle. " What happened coming home ? Did you sit with your back to the engine then ? "

" Yes," said Mister Widdle.

" But, Widdle, you are foolish ! " cried Mrs. Widdle crossly. " Why didn't you change places with the person opposite you again ? "

" I am *not* foolish ! " said Mister Widdle, his nose in the air. " I *would* have changed places—but there was nobody there to change places with ! "

Then, to Mister Widdle's surprise, Mrs. Widdle began to laugh and laugh and laugh. " Oh ! " she said, wiping her tears away, " you are even more foolish than I thought you were ! "

Poor Mister Widdle couldn't *think* why. Can you ?

Who Stole the Crown?

THE King of Pixieland had two crowns. One was a summer crown, made of gold, light and easy to wear. The other was also made of gold, but it had a warm winter lining of red velvet, for the pixie King suffered from cold ears.

In the winter-time, when the King wore his warm crown, the summer crown was placed in a safe place, locked up in a box in the middle of a hollow tree. Nobody knew where it was except the King himself, and Pointy, the keeper of the crown.

One wintry day, when Pointy went to get out the summer crown to give it a polish-up, he found it was gone! Goodness, what a state he was in! He looked up and down the hollow tree, he ran all round it in the thick snow—for it was a bitterly cold winter's day and snowing hard—and he looked everywhere he could think of. But it was no use; the crown was gone.

" Oh, oh, oh, it's gone!" cried Pointy, in a great way. " It's been stolen! Who did it? Who did it?"

He ran to the King and told him. The King sent his soldiers to hunt through the wood, but all in vain. The golden crown was gone.

" What shall I do when summer comes?" wondered the King. " I can't wear *this* heavy crown—and I can't afford to buy another. Dear me, this is very annoying. I wonder who could have found my crown and stolen it. If I knew the thief I could go and search his house and see if the crown was there."

"Your Majesty," said Pointy, suddenly, "you have heard of Little-cap, the pixie, I expect? Well, folk say he is very clever indeed. Shall we ask him to come here and find out the thief for us? He boasts that he can solve any mystery, so maybe he can help us."

"Send for him at once," ordered the King. So Little-cap was sent for, and he came. He was a funny little pixie. The King looked at him and wondered if he even knew that twice times two were four, he was so little and so babyish.

He was dressed in a yellow tunic with green buttons, and on his head was a funny little cap of yellow, with bells all round it. They tinkled whenever Little-cap thought hard, and were silent when he wasn't thinking about anything much.

Little-cap took off his hat when he came before the King, for it was not polite to keep it on. He bowed very low and went red with excitement.

"I hear you can solve mysteries," said the King.

"Well, I have tried to," said Little-cap. "Most mysteries are easy to solve if you think about them hard enough. Have *you* a mystery for me to solve?"

"Yes," said the King, and he told Little-cap about his stolen crown. The pixie listened without saying a word.

"Now," said the King, when the tale was told, "can you find out who stole my crown?"

"Yes, I think so," said the pixie, smiling all over his babyish face. "I just want to know a few things first."

"Ask any question you like," said the King.

Little-cap put on his hat and thought hard. All the bells rang loudly.

"First," said Little-cap, "please tell me the names of all who live in the wood where you kept your crown."

Pointy stepped forward and told the pixie all who lived in the wood.

"There is Prickles, the hedgehog," he said. "There is Bushy, the squirrel. There is Dozy, the dormouse, and Sly-one, the snake. There is Crawler, the toad, and Hopper, the frog, who lives in the pond in the middle of the wood. And there is Floppy, the rabbit, too, of course, and all the little folk as well. But they had all gone to a party that day and the wood was empty of them. So you can rule out any of the little folk. It was one of the four-footed creatures—but which one?"

"It's a puzzle," said the King, sighing.

Little-cap thought again, and all the bells on his hat jingled merrily.

"One more question," he said. "What sort of a day was it when the crown was stolen?"

"Oh, the weather was terribly bad," said the King, shivering. "I remember the day well because my ears were cold even under my red velvet crown. It was snowing hard and there was a bitter wind. That was why we couldn't see any footprints, you see—because the snow was falling and had covered up any marks."

"I see, I see," said Little-cap, and he put his head down upon his chest. Once more the bells on his hat rang loudly and cheerfully.

"It's a terrible puzzle, isn't it?" said the King. "I'm afraid it's too deep a mystery for you, Little-cap."

"Not at all," said the pixie, raising his head and looking at the King with a smile. "It's easy. I was only just wondering why the thief took your crown, because it would look so silly on him."

"What! Do you know who the thief was?" cried the King, in astonishment.

"Oh yes," said Little-cap. "Of course I do."

"But how do you know?" asked the King, only half believing him. "Why, you haven't even been to look at the tree or the wood or anything!"

"I don't need to," said Little-cap, getting up from his seat. "Why, Your Majesty, if you thought for a few moments about what you have just told me, *you* would know who was the thief, too."

"Well, who *is* the thief?" asked the King, impatiently.

"Floppy, the rabbit," said Little-cap. "Send your soldiers to look through his burrow. The crown will be there."

Pointy at once sent off six soldiers to Floppy's burrow. The rabbit was sitting just inside and when he saw the soldiers, his nose began to woffle up and down in fright.

"W-w-w-w-what do you w-w-w-want?" he said.

"We've come to search your burrow," said the Captain. "See, here is a note from the King to give us permission."

He showed the frightened rabbit the King's scribbled order and Floppy shook from whiskers to tail.

"We've come to find the crown you stole from the hollow tree," said the Captain. "If you'll tell us where you've put it, we needn't turn your burrow upside-down."

Then the rabbit began to cry loudly, and woffled his nose so fast that the soldiers could hardly see it.

"It's in my b-b-b-b-bedroom!" stammered the rabbit,

miserably, weeping big tears down his whiskers. "I'll go and get it."

"No, you won't," said the Captain, catching hold of the rabbit firmly. "I know you rabbits—you're in at one hole and out at the other before anyone can wink an eye! Yes, you'd just whip up the crown and run off before anyone could stop you! You stay here and I'll send a couple of soldiers to your bedroom."

Two soldiers went down the burrow. They soon came to the big hole where the rabbit slept. It was lined with dry grass and leaves and was a cosy, warm place. Under the leaves was the crown! Yes, really, there it was, dazzling bright, the King's beautiful summer crown.

The rabbit and the crown were both taken to the King. He was delighted to see his crown, and he frowned angrily at the wicked rabbit.

"Take him to the castle and lock him up underground," he ordered.

"Oh no," said Little-cap, the pixie. "Don't do that! Put him in the highest tower!"

"Why?" asked the King, in astonishment.

"Because rabbits love to be underground," answered Little-cap. "Floppy will simply dig a tunnel and escape! But put him in a high tower and he'll be safe!"

So the rabbit was marched off to a high tower. Then the King turned to Little-cap and begged him to explain how he had solved the mystery in such a short time.

"Well," said the pixie, with a laugh, "I knew it was Floppy, because the rabbit was the only one of those seven creatures out that day."

"How do you know that?" asked the King. "How do you know it wasn't Dozy, the dormouse, or Sly-one, the snake?"

"Because the dormouse sleeps hard all the winter through and never wakes, and the snake sleeps too, curled up with his

brothers in the tree at the edge of the wood," said Little-cap. "Dormice and snakes are never about in the winter."

"Well, what about Hopper, the frog?" said the King.

"The frog always sleeps in the pond during the winter," said the pixie. "It was frozen over that day, so it couldn't have been Hopper, even if he had waked up."

"Why couldn't it have been Crawler, the toad?" asked Pointy.

"The toad crawls under a stone and goes to sleep in the cold weather," said Little-cap, smiling. "He never wakes up till the spring-time. All toads and frogs sleep the winter through."

"Well, Bushy, the squirrel, and Prickles, the hedgehog, don't sleep all the winter through," said the King. "It might have been them, mightn't it? Bushy is often out on a sunny winter's day, looking for the nuts he hid in the autumn—

and as for Prickles, I've sometimes met him snuffling about the ditches on a warm night in winter!"

"Quite right," said Little-cap, nodding his head. "Quite right—but you will remember, Your Majesty, that Pointy said it was bad weather with a bitter wind when the crown was stolen, and both squirrels and hedgehogs curl themselves up tighter than ever and sleep deeply in weather like that. So it couldn't have been them."

"Well," said the King, thinking hard, "well, that only leaves Floppy the rabbit."

"Exactly," said the pixie, with a grin. "That's just what I thought! And I was right! It's quite easy to solve a mystery when you think hard enough, isn't it, Your Majesty!"

And off he went, humming a little tune, while all the bells on his hat tinkled and rang.

"Well, well!" said the King. "We might have been just as clever as Little-cap, if we'd thought!"

"But we *didn't* think!" said Pointy.

"Tell Me My Name!"

THE Hoppetty Gnome lived in a little cottage all by himself. He kept no dog and no cat, but outside in the garden lived a fat, freckled thrush who sang to Hoppetty each morning and evening to thank him for the crumbs he put out.

Hoppetty was very fond of this thrush. She was a pretty bird, and the songs she sang were very lovely.

> "The sky is blue, blue!
> And all day through, through,
> I sing to you, you!"

That was the thrush's favourite song, and Hoppetty knew it by heart.

Now one day a dreadful thing happened. Hoppetty was trotting through the wood, going home after his shopping, when out pounced a big black goblin and caught hold of him. He put little Hoppetty into a sack and ran off with the struggling gnome over hill and meadow until he came to the tall hill on the top of which he lived. Then he emptied Hoppetty out of his sack, and told him he was to be his cook.

"I am very fond of cakes with jam inside," said the grinning goblin, "and I love chocolate fingers sprinkled with nut. I have heard that you are a clever cake-maker. Make me these things."

Poor Hoppetty! How he had to work! The goblin really had a most enormous appetite, and as he ate nothing but jam cakes and chocolate fingers, Hoppetty was busy all day long

at the oven, baking, baking. He was always hot and always tired. He wondered and wondered who this strange goblin was, and one day he asked him.

"Who are you, Master?" he said.

"Oho! Wouldn't you like to know?" said the goblin, putting six chocolate fingers into his mouth at once. "Well, Hoppetty, if you could guess my name, I'd let you go. But you never will!"

Hoppetty sighed. He was sure he never *would* guess the goblin's name. Goblins had such strange names. Nobody ever came to the house, no letters were pushed through the letter-box, and Hoppetty was never allowed to go out. So how could he possibly find out the goblin's name? He tried a few guesses.

"Is your name Thingumebob?"

"Ho, ho, ho! No, no, no!"

"Is it Mankypetoddle?"

"Ho, ho, ho! No, no, no!"

"Well, is it Tiddleywinks?"

"Ho, ho, ho! No, no, no!"

Then Hoppetty sighed and set to work to make more jam cakes, for the goblin had eaten twenty-two for breakfast, and the larder was getting empty.

The goblin went out and banged the door. He locked it too, and went down the path. Hoppetty knew he couldn't get out. He had tried before. The windows opened two inches, and no more. The door he couldn't open at all. He was indeed a prisoner. He sighed again and set to work quickly.

And then he heard something that made his heart leap. It was a bird singing sweetly.

> "The sky is blue, blue!
> And all day through, through,
> I sing to you, you!"

It was his thrush! Hoppetty rushed to the window and looked out of the open crack. There was the pretty freckled bird, sitting in a nearby tree.

"Thrush!" cried Hoppetty. "I'm here! Oh, you dear creature, have you been going about singing and looking for me? Did you miss your crumbs? I'm a prisoner here. I can only get away if I find out the name of the goblin who keeps me here."

Just then the goblin came back, and the gnome rushed to his baking once more. The thrush sang sweetly outside for a few minutes and then flew away.

The bird was unhappy. It loved little Hoppetty. The gnome had been so kind to her, and had loved her singing so very much. If only the thrush could find out the name of the goblin. But how?

The bird made up her mind to watch the goblin and see where he went. So the next day she followed him when he left the cottage, flying from tree to tree as the goblin went on his way. At last he came to another cottage, and, to the thrush's surprise, the door was opened by a black cat with bright green eyes.

"A witch cat!" thought the thrush. "I wonder if she knows the goblin's name. I dare not ask her, for if I go too near she will spring at me."

The goblin stayed a little while and then went away. The thrush was about to follow, when the cat brought out a spinning-wheel and set it in the sunshine by the door. She sat down and began to spin her wool.

And as she spun, she sang a strange song.

> "First of eel, and second of hen,
>   And after that the fourth of wren.
> Third of lean and first of meat,
> Second of leg and third of feet.
> Fifth of strong and second of pail,
> Fourth of hammer and third of nail.
> Sixth of button and third of coat,
> First of me and second of boat.
> When you've played this curious game,
> You may perchance have found his name!"

The cat sang this over and over again, and the thrush listened hard. Soon she knew it by heart and at once flew off to the goblin's cottage. She put her head on one side and looked in at the window. Hoppetty was setting the table for the goblin and was talking to him.

"Is your name Twisty-tail?"

"Ho, ho, ho! No, no, no!" roared the goblin.

"Well, is it Twisty-nose?"

"Ho, ho, ho! No, no, no! And don't you be rude!" snapped the goblin.

"Well, is it Pointed-ears?" asked poor Hoppetty.

"Ho, ho, ho! No, no, no! Give me some more jam cakes!" ordered the goblin.

The next day the thrush waited until the goblin had gone out, and then she began to sing sweetly.

Hoppetty knew that it was his own thrush singing, and he went to the window and listened—but what a peculiar song the bird was whistling! The thrush sang the cat's song over and over again—and suddenly Hoppetty guessed that it was trying to tell him how to find the goblin's name. He frowned and thought hard. Yes—he thought he could!

He fetched a pencil and a piece of paper and sat down. The thrush flew to the window-sill and sang the song slowly. Hoppetty put down the words and then he began to work out the puzzle in great excitement.

"The first of eel—that's E. The second of hen—that's E too. The fourth of wren—that's N. The third of lean—A. The first of meat—M. Second of leg—another E. Third of feet—E again! Fifth of strong, that's N. Second of pail—A. Fourth of hammer—M. Third of nail—I. Sixth of button—N. Third of coat—A. First of me—M, and second of coat—O! Now what do all these letters spell?"

He wrote the letters out in a word, and looked at it— EENA-MEENA-MINA-MO!

"So that's the goblin's name!" cried the gnome in excitement. "Oh, I would never, never have thought of that!"

The thrush flew off in a hurry, for she heard the goblin returning. He strode into his cottage and scowled when he saw the gnome sitting down writing instead of baking.

"What's all this?" he roared.

"Is your name Tabby-cat?" asked the gnome, with a grin.

"Ho, ho, ho! No, no, no!" cried the goblin. "Get to your work."

"Is it—is it—Wibbly-Wobbly?" asked the gnome, pretending to be frightened.

"Ho, ho, ho! No, no, no!" shouted the goblin in a rage. "Where are my jam cakes?"

"Is it—can it be—EENA-MEENA-MINA-MO?" cried the gnome suddenly.

The goblin stared at Hoppetty and turned pale. "How do you know that?" he asked, in a frightened whisper. "No one knows it! No one! Now you have found out my secret name! Oh! Oh! Go, you horrid creature! I am afraid of you! What will you find out next?"

He flung the door wide open, and Hoppetty ran out gladly, shouting :

> " Eena, Meena, Mina, Mo,
> Catch a goblin by his toe;
> If he squeals, let him go,
> Eena, Meena, Mina, Mo ! "

He skipped all the way home—and there, sitting on his garden gate, was his friend the thrush. You can guess that Hoppetty gave her a fine meal of crumbs, and told her all about how angry and frightened the goblin was !

" I shall bake you a cake for yourself every time I have a baking day," he promised. And he did—but, as you can guess, he never again made a jam cake or a chocolate finger !

Gooseberry Whiskers

THERE was once a rascally gnome who sold fine paint-brushes to the fairies. No brushes were half as good as his, for the hairs in them were so fine and strong.

"Where do you get them from?" asked the elves one day. But the gnome wouldn't tell them.

"It's a secret," he said. "Perhaps I make them out of moonbeams drawn out long and thin, and snipped off in short pieces!"

"You don't!" cried the elves. "Oh *do* tell us your secret!"

But he never would—and the reason was that he was afraid to. He got the hairs from sleeping caterpillars, and such a thing was not allowed in Fairyland, as you may guess. Many caterpillars were covered with soft fine hairs, and by pulling a few from this one and a few from that, the little gnome soon had enough for a new brush.

One spring-cleaning time there was a great demand for his brushes. All through May the elves came to buy from him and the gnome could hardly find enough caterpillars to pull hairs from!

He began to pull more than a few hairs from each. Once he took quite a handful, and the caterpillar woke up with a squeak.

Another furry caterpillar woke up one morning to find that he was quite bald. He hadn't a single hair left and he shivered with cold.

When the Queen passed by she stopped in surprise.

"But who could have taken your hairs away?" she asked the caterpillar. "No one would do such a naughty thing."

"Please, Your Majesty, someone must have done it last night," said the caterpillar.

"And half *my* coat is gone too!" said another.

"And about thirty of my finest hairs have disappeared as well!" cried a third.

"This must be looked into," said the Queen, sternly.

She called to her guards and spoke to them. "Twelve of you must remain here to look after these caterpillars," she

commanded. "You can hide under the hedge, and watch for the thief. Catch him and punish him well."

The caterpillars crawled to their leaves. Now at last they would be safe! The twelve guards looked about for good hiding-places, and then played a game of snap until night-time, for they felt sure there would be no sign of the thief until darkness fell. The caterpillars were so interested in the game that they called "Snap!" when they shouldn't, and made the guards quite cross.

"Don't interfere," said the captain. "*We* are playing, not you. You eat your juicy leaves, and don't disturb us or we will leave you to the robber!"

When night came the soldiers squeezed themselves into their hiding-places and kept watch. The night was dark, and it was difficult for them to see an inch in front of their noses. Just the night for a robber to come!

Time went on. No thief. Ten o'clock came, eleven o'clock. Still no thief. The guards began to yawn. Surely the robber would not come now.

But at that very moment the little gnome was out on his rounds, looking for furry caterpillars. He was hunting under the leaves, down the stalks, on the ground, and everywhere. He didn't know that anyone was lying in wait for him.

He was very silent. His feet made no sound as he crept along, and he didn't even rustle a leaf.

"Where are all the caterpillars to-night?" he thought. "I can't seem to find any!"

From bush to bush he went, feeling along the leaves, and at last he really did find a large furry caterpillar, peacefully sleeping.

" Good ! " thought the gnome. " This one has a fine crop of hairs ! I can make a fine brush from them."

He grabbed a big handful from the back of the sleeping caterpillar, and pulled hard. The caterpillar woke up with a loud squeak. " Eee, eee, eee ! " it cried.

At once all the guards sprang up and shouted loudly. " The robber, the robber ! "

The gnome fled away in terror, holding all the hairs in his hand. The guards ran after him, and went crashing through the woods into the palace gardens. Up and down the paths they went, searching for the thief. Where was he ? Where had he gone ?

The little gnome had found a prickly hiding-place under a big gooseberry bush. He crouched there in fright, wondering what would happen to him if he was found. In his hand he still held the caterpillar hairs. Whatever could he do with them ?

" The guards mustn't find them in my hand," he thought. " And I daren't throw them away, for they are sure to be found. What *can* I do ? "

He put out his hand and felt about. He touched two or three big fat gooseberries—and then an idea came to him. He would stick the hairs on them, for surely no one would think of looking on the fruit for caterpillar hairs !

In a trice he was sticking the hairs on the green smooth surface of the gooseberries. He made them all hairy and whiskery, and just as he had finished, somebody came down the path near-by, and flashed a lantern on to him.

" Here's someone ! " they cried. " Here's the thief ! Quick, come and get him ! "

The gnome was dragged out and searched. No hairs were found on him, but in his pocket were two brushes that he had forgotten about—and they were made of caterpillar hairs !

" Spank him, spank him well ! " cried the captain. " That will teach him not to steal ! Then turn him out of Fairyland for ever ! "

So the gnome was spanked very hard, and taken to the gates of Fairyland. They were shut be-hind him, and out he went, weeping bitterly.

No one has heard of him since—but from that day to this gooseberries have always grown whiskers. If you don't believe me, go and look for yourself !

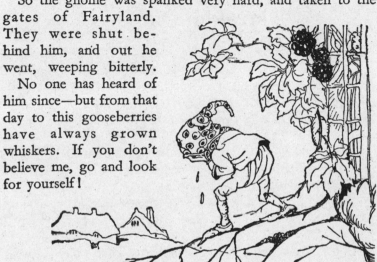

The Mean Old Man

ONCE upon a time there was a mean old man who wouldn't pay his bills. He owed Dame Rustle a lot of money for his newspapers. He owed Mr. Pork shillings and shillings for his meat. Mother Cluck sent him in a bill for milk and eggs time after time, but it was never paid. Really, it was dreadful!

One day they all put their heads together and laid a little plan. They bought a come-back spell from Witch Heyho and took bits of it back to their shops.

And the next day, when Dame Rustle gave a newspaper to old Mister Mean, she tucked a bit of the come-back spell into it. When Mr. Pork sold him a string of sausages, he tucked a come-back spell into them too, and when Mother Cluck let Mister Mean have a basket of new-laid eggs she carefully put a come-back spell at the bottom.

Well, old Mister Mean set off home, carrying the basket of eggs, the sausages in paper, and the morning newspaper. But before he had got very far a curious thing happened. The come-back spell began to work!

It worked on the newspaper first. The paper grew small legs and tried to get away from under Mister Mean's arm! Mister Mean could not think why it kept slipping. He kept pushing it back under his arm—but still that newspaper wriggled and wriggled and at last it fell to the ground. No sooner did it feel its feet there than it tore off down the pavement as fast as it could go, running back to Dame Rustle's!

"Gracious!" said Mister Mean in surprise. "How the wind is taking that paper along, to be sure."

Well, the next thing that happened was most annoying to Mister Mean. The come-back spell began to work in the sausages, and they wriggled out of their paper wrapping, which fell to the ground. Mister Mean stopped to pick it up—and, hey presto! that string of sausages leapt to the ground and tore off on tiny legs as fast as could be. All the dogs in the street barked to see them rushing along like a large brown caterpillar—but they knew better than to touch sausages with a come-back spell in them.

"Jumping pigs!" said Mister Mean in the greatest alarm. "Now, what's the meaning of that? Look at those sausages! Do they think they are in for a race or what? Something funny is about this morning—or else I'm dreaming!"

He pinched himself hard to see if he was dreaming—but the pinch hurt so much that he knew he was wide awake. So on he went again, wondering what could be the matter with everything.

"Anyhow, the eggs are all right," he said, looking down at them. But even as he spoke the come-back spell began to work in them, too. One by one those eggs grew chicken-legs and climbed up to the rim of the basket, ready to jump out!

"Oh no, you don't!" said Mister Mean, grabbing at the top egg. "No jumping about like that, eggs, or you will get broken."

But the eggs took no notice of Mister Mean. One by one they jumped out of the basket and tore back to Mother Cluck's as fast as they could. It was a most astonishing sight to see.

Mister Mean was furious. "There's some spell at work," he cried. "Someone's playing a trick on me!"

"Perhaps, Mister Mean," said Mrs. Twinkle-toes, who was just nearby, "perhaps you haven't paid for those things. They have gone back to be sold to someone who *will* pay for them."

Mister Mean went home in a rage. He wasn't going to pay his bills till he wanted to. Nobody could make him take his money out of the bank if he didn't mean to!

But, oh dear! what a life he led the next few days! His new hat jumped clean off his head and hurried back to the hatter's. His new shoes wriggled off his feet and ran back to the shoe shop with such a clatter that everyone turned to see what was making the noise—and of course they saw old Mister Mean standing in his stockinged feet looking as wild as could be—and, dear me, he had such a big hole in one toe.

Even the bananas he bought hopped out of the bag they were in and galloped back to the greengrocer's. Soon the people of the town followed Mister Mean when he did his shopping, so that they could see the strange sight of everything racing back to the shops afterwards.

Well, Mister Mean knew there was nothing else to be done but to pay his bills. So he took some money out of the bank and paid them all, every one. Then his goods stopped behaving in such a queer manner and stayed in their bags and baskets till he got home.

And you may be sure they will behave all right just so long

as he pays his bills—but as the shopkeepers still have some of the come-back spell left, they will play old Mister Mean some more tricks if he begins to be mean again.

Witch Heyho still has plenty of come-back spells to sell, so if you know of anyone who needs one, just send a message to her!

Good Old Jumbo!

OUTSIDE the nursery window lived three small pixies called Binks, Jinks and Dimple. The toys knew them very well indeed, for the pixies came into the nursery every night when it was dark, and played with them.

Binks and Jinks were big strong pixies, but Dimple was small and sweet. She was their sister, and they loved her very much. All the toys were good to her and she rode in the wooden train, in the toy motor car and in the clockwork train as many times as she liked.

She liked all the toys except big Jumbo, the grey elephant. He had once trodden on her toe by accident, and she was frightened of him. He was so big and clumsy. Jumbo was sad about it, because he liked Dimple very much, and was always longing to give her a ride on his back. But she never would ride on him.

The toys belonged to two children, Amy and Michael. But lately the children hadn't bothered at all about their toys, because Uncle Jim had given them something they liked much better—two pairs of roller skates! You should have seen how Amy and Michael tore round and round the garden paths on their skates! Goodness, they went like lightning!

The toys were jealous of the roller skates. The children kept them in the toy cupboard but every night the toys pushed them out. They didn't like them.

"They are nasty things," said the golliwog. "I don't know why the children like them better than they like us. Get out of the toy cupboard, you ugly things! You don't belong here!"

Then bump-bump! Out would tumble the four skates on to the floor. They weren't alive, so they didn't mind one way or another. But the children were always puzzled to know how it was their skates fell out of the toy cupboard so often!

The toys played by themselves each night, and were very glad when the three pixies came to join them.

"It's nice to have *somebody* to play with," said the teddy bear. "The children hardly ever take any notice of us now!"

One night Binks and Jinks came in at the window in a great hurry, looking as scared as could be.

"Toys, toys! What shall we do? Six red goblins came to-night and stole away Dimple, our little pixie sister! Oh, whatever shall we do?"

The toys turned pale with fright. Even the golliwog looked quite white, so you can guess how frightened they all were. The red goblins were nasty creatures, with claws instead of nails and they could scratch just like cats.

"We could never catch up with the goblins!" said the golliwog. "They go so fast!"

"Well, you can't ask *me* to go after them," said the clock-work train, in a hurry. "I can only run on my rails."

"And my key is lost," said the clockwork motor car. "*I* can't go!"

"Nobody wants to go!" wailed the two pixies sorrowfully. "Poor Dimple! She'll never come back again."

Then the big elephant, Jumbo, spoke in his big deep voice. "*I* will go and chase those goblins!" he said. "*I'm* not afraid!"

"But dear old Jumbo, you're so slow and clumsy!" cried all the toys together.

"Ah, but I've got a splendid idea!" said Jumbo. "I want you to strap those roller skates on to my big feet. Then I shall go like the wind, roller-skating all down the paths to Goblin-Land!"

Well, what an idea! Did you ever hear anything like it! I never did. Anyway, you should have seen how the toys and the two pixies clapped their hands when they heard what Jumbo said. They thought it was the best idea they had ever heard.

"Quick! Get the roller skates!" cried Binks and Jinks. "Where are they?"

Golly got one, teddy bear found another, and the two biggest dolls brought the last two. Then they strapped them on to Jumbo's big, clumsy feet. He *did* look funny!

"I'm just going to have a skate round the nursery to see if I can do it properly," said Jumbo, shaking with excitement. Crash-crash-crash went his feet, as he tried his hardest to skate with all four at once. Dear me, you should have seen him!

All the toys got out of his way in a great hurry, for his four feet shot out all over the place, and he didn't know at all where he was going. He knocked the golliwog down flat on his nose and ran over the teddy bear's big toe. Goodness, it was a sight to see!

"Steady on, Jumbo!" called Binks, jumping up on to a chair for safety. "Oh, good gracious!"

Jumbo bounced into the chair and sent it flying! Down fell poor Binks with a crash. Up he got and climbed up on to the window-sill, feeling certain that Jumbo couldn't knock *that* down!

After a little while Jumbo began to skate much better. His legs went properly and he found that he could skate right round the nursery and back again without falling over once. He did feel proud.

"Now I'm ready to go after Dimple and the goblins," he said to the pixies. "Jump up on my back and tell me the right way to go."

Binks and Jinks jumped up on to his broad back, and hung on tightly. Crash-crash-crash went the roller skates as Jumbo skated out of the room and down the passage to the garden. What a noise he made! It's a wonder nobody heard him!

The moon was shining brightly. Down the garden path went Jumbo, skating splendidly. If one of his feet slipped he still had three others to help him, so he didn't fall over at all.

He *did* go at a rate! Out into the lane he skated and over the hill. Then down a large rabbit-hole to Goblin-Land.

The streets of Goblin-Land are very straight and smooth, so Jumbo found he could go at top speed there! Crash-crash-crash went his skates and he tore along faster than any motor car could possibly go. Binks and Jinks soon lost their hats, for the wind streamed past them and snatched away their hats with greedy fingers.

"There they are, there they are!" suddenly shouted Binks, so loudly that he frightened Jinks and nearly made him fall off Jumbo's back. Jumbo looked in front of him and saw a crowd of little red goblins riding yellow rocking-horses. One of them held Dimple tightly in his arms, whilst he shouted to his rocking-horse to rock faster and faster through Goblin-Land.

Jumbo made a sound like a trumpet and skated on faster than ever. The goblins heard the crash of his roller skates and looked back. When they saw Jumbo behind them on skates, carrying Binks and Jinks on his back, they could hardly believe their eyes. They whipped their rocking-horses and shouted to them loudly.

"Go on! Go on! Faster still! Hurry, hurry, hurry!"

The rocking-horses rocked away till it seemed as if they must tumble on their noses or tails. They went very fast indeed. But Jumbo went even faster. How he skated! You could hardly see his legs moving, they went so quickly.

"They're taking Dimple to the Deep Green Cave!" suddenly cried Binks. "Oh dear, catch them before they get there, Jumbo, or we shall never see our dear little sister again!"

Sure enough, the goblins were going to the Deep Green Cave. Jumbo saw the mountain in which it was, and he skated even faster to get there before the goblins did—and he got there at exactly the same minute. Then you should have seen him fighting those goblins with his skates! First this skate

hit a goblin and then that one. Binks and Jinks joined in too and fought the goblins bravely, though they scratched just like cats.

"Let's go and get the green goblins to help us!" suddenly shouted a red goblin to his friends. So they all rushed into the Deep Green Cave to get help, and left Dimple, Binks and Jinks with Jumbo outside.

"On my back, quick, all of you!" shouted Jumbo, in his trumpeting voice. Binks and Jinks jumped up, and helped Dimple. She had quite forgotten that she had said she never, never would ride on Jumbo, but got up as quickly as ever she could.

Then back went Jumbo, skating as fast as his four legs would take him. Long before the green and the red goblins came running out of their cave Jumbo was out of sight, crash-crash-crashing along on his four roller skates !

It didn't take him long to get back to the nursery, very much out of breath, but simply delighted with himself. He had got dear little Dimple on his back at last ! The toys gave him a great welcome, and cheered him with all their might. His trunk blushed quite red with pride.

The toys unstrapped the skates from his tired feet and put them away again. Then they heard the first cock crowing to say that day was coming, so they hurriedly said good-bye to the pixies and climbed back into the toy cupboard to go to sleep.

Binks and Jinks patted Jumbo before they went, but Dimple flung her arms round his trunk and kissed him lovingly.

"You're a dear, brave Jumbo," she said, "and I'm sorry I ever said you were clumsy. I'll come and ride on you every single night if you'll let me ! "

Then off she went, and left Jumbo standing by himself, very happy indeed.

The Nice Juicy Carrot

IN THE field at the back of the farm lived three grey donkeys. They were called Neddy, Biddy, and Hee-Haw. Sometimes the farmer put one into the harness belonging to a small carriage, and his little daughter drove out for a ride. But usually the donkeys didn't have much to do, and they very often quarrelled.

One day Neddy found a large juicy carrot in the ditch, and he was most excited about it. In fact, he was so excited that instead of keeping quiet about it and nibbling it till it was gone, he raised his head and cried: "Eeyore! Eeyore! Eeyore!"

Just like that.

Well, of course, the other two donkeys came running up to see what was the matter, and they saw the nice juicy carrot too. And they wanted to eat it.

But Neddy put his thick little body in the way and said :
" No, that's my carrot."

Biddy tried to scrape the carrot near her with her foot.

" It's *my* carrot ! " she said.

" I'm the hungriest, so it's *my* carrot ! " said Hee-Haw, and
he tried to push the others away.

Then Neddy saw that he would not be allowed to eat it in
peace, and he thought of a plan to decide which donkey should
have the carrot. " Let us see who can bray the loudest," he
said.

So they began. First Neddy brayed.

" Eeyore, eeyore, eeyore ! " he cried, and a little sandy
rabbit running not far off was so astonished at the loud noise
that he came near to see what it was all about.

Then Biddy brayed. " EEYORE, EEYORE, EEYORE ! " she
cried, and the watching rabbit thought it a very ugly noise.

Then Hee-Haw brayed, and dear me, his voice was so loud
that a hedgehog not far off was frightened almost out of his
life, and curled himself up into a tight ball.

" EEYORE, EEYORE, EEYORE ! " roared Hee-Haw.
The listening rabbit thought that donkeys had terrible voices.
Then, dear me, the rabbit caught sight of that nice juicy carrot
lying just nearby in the ditch. How his nose woffled when
he saw it !

He crept out from his hiding-place and the three donkeys
saw him.

" Look ! There is a rabbit ! " cried Hee-Haw. " He shall
tell us which brayed the loudest just now. Then we shall
know who wins the carrot ! "

So they called to the rabbit to judge between them. But
the bunny was very artful. He didn't want to see the carrot
eaten by a donkey. So he looked wisely at the three grey
animals and shook his head.

" There wasn't much to choose between your braying," he

said. " Why don't you have a race ? Then you could easily
tell who should have the carrot."

" That's a good idea," said the donkeys. " Where shall we
race to, rabbit ? "

" Oh, all round the field and back again to where I sit,"
answered the wily rabbit. " Now, are you ready ? One, two,
three, off ! "

Away went the three donkeys at top speed. Round the field
they went at a gallop, much to the astonishment of the farmer's
wife. They panted and puffed, kicking up their heels in fine
style, each trying to get ahead of the other.

They all arrived back at the starting-place at the same
moment. But each donkey thought it had won.

" I've won ! " said Neddy.

" No, I'm first ! " brayed Biddy.

" The carrot's mine ! " roared Hee-Haw.

" Let's ask the rabbit who's won," said Neddy. " He'll
know."

So they called to the rabbit—but there was no answer. They
called again, and still they had no reply. Then they looked
for the carrot.

It was gone !

The Dandelion Clock

ONCE upon a time there was a fine dandelion plant that lived in a field. It put up many flowers—but one after another they were eaten by the brown horses that slept in the field each night.

At last the dandelion plant put up a golden flower bigger and finer than any before. The horses did not eat it, for they had found some very juicy grass at the other end of the field, and they did not visit the hedge where the dandelion lived. So the flower grew tall.

The bees came to it. So did many little flies. The flower lasted for five whole days, and then it closed its pretty petals and hid its head in its green leaves. It stayed hidden there for a few days, and then once more it straightened out its long stalk, which had grown even taller. And lo and behold, the dandelion's golden head had turned white! All the gold had gone.

"You do look different," said a little copper beetle, hurrying by.

"My head is full of seed now, precious seed!" said the dandelion. "I have thirty-one seeds to send away on the wind —and that means, little beetle, thirty-one new dandelion plants!"

"Wonderful!" said the beetle, and ran down a hole.

The dandelion head fluffed itself out into a beautiful clock. You should have seen it! It was round and white and soft, like a full, silvery moon. It stood there shining softly in the hedge, waiting for the wind to come and puff all the seeds away.

But before the wind came someone else came—and that was

a little girl. She saw the dandelion clock there and she squealed in delight.

"What a beautiful clock! I must blow it to tell the time!" So she picked the clock and began to puff.

"One o'clock! Two o'clock! Three o'clock! Oh! The fluff is all gone. It's three o'clock!"

The little girl threw away the stalk and went dancing away. And what happened to all the seeds?

A pretty goldfinch came by and saw them blowing away, all the thirty-one. He twittered to his companions, and the flock came flying down. "Dandelion seeds!" sang the goldfinch. "Take them, brothers! We have feasted on thistledown to-day, and now here are some dandelion seeds."

They ate all they could see—twenty of them! Then off they flew. Now there were only eleven of the seeds left. "Never mind!" sighed the plant, and it rustled its leaves together. "That will be eleven new plants some day."

The eleven seeds flew off. Each tiny seed had a little parachute to help it to fly. They swung through the air, enjoying the sunshine and the wind. Two flew down to earth to look for a resting-place, but a little mouse was there and he caught them. He ate the seeds and then carried the fluff to his nest to make it cosy. So now there were only nine left.

The nine seeds flew on and on, over the fields and hedges. Three floated downwards—and a tiny pixie caught them and sewed them on to her pointed cap. They made a lovely trimming and she was very pleased with it.

Now there were only six seeds, and they floated high on the wind. Two flew into a squirrel's hole and caught on the bark of the tree. The squirrel saw them and licked them off. Down his throat they went, and that left only four—four little dandelion seeds, adventuring through the air, blown up and down and round about by all the autumn breezes!

One fell to earth and was eaten by a brown sparrow.

Another fell down a chimney and was burnt in the fire. Now there were only two left.

They floated onwards. One came to a pond and fell there. A fish saw it floating on the water, its little parachute looking like wings—and the fish thought the seed was a fly, and snapped at it. That was the end of that little seed. Only one was left. It flew for a long while, soaring up high, and then sinking down low.

And at last it rested on the ground, a tiny, tired seed, its parachute falling to bits. It lay there, not moving, for there was now no wind at all. It was just outside a worm-hole. That night the worm came out of its hole and wriggled about on the grass. When it went back again it glided over the dandelion seed, and the tiny seed stuck to the worm's slimy body. It went into the hole with the worm.

And there it grew! Yes—it really did! It put out a little root. It put out a tiny green shoot—and when the spring came, there was a small dandelion plant growing out of the worm-hole!

"Now, how did that dandelion get there?" wondered the little girl in whose garden the worm-hole was. "I like dandelions. I shall let it grow and give me some golden flowers."

So the dandelion grew, and was happy and content in the warm spring sunshine and soft rain. And before long it had seven fine white clocks, all ready to be puffed.

The little girl puffed them—and off went the seed. I wonder if any will fall in your garden? Perhaps they will—and you will see a tiny plant growing up, and find golden flowers, as round as pennies, shining in the sun!

King Bom's Ice-Cream

KING BOM was a perfect nuisance. He was a very stupid fellow, but he thought he was clever, so he was always interfering in everything and making muddles. People got very tired of him, especially his wife, Queen Prylla, who often used to long to box his ears. But she didn't dare to in case Bom ordered her head to be cut off.

That was one of his very stupid habits. He would say " Off with his head ! " at any time, and, although he might be very sorry the next day, by that time, of course, it was too late to change his mind.

One day King Bom went to a meeting of his councillors, and upset all their plans. No matter what they proposed to do he wanted something different. In the end all the councillors walked out in a huff, and the King roared, " Off with their heads ! "

" You can't do that," said the Queen quickly. " The people will rise against you if you do, and put you off the throne."

" Off with *their* heads then ! " roared the King, losing his temper even more.

" Don't be silly," said the Queen sharply. " If you cut off everybody's head you won't have any people to rule over and you won't like that ! "

The King stared so fiercely at Queen Prylla that she quite thought he would say " Off with her head ! " too. So she went up to him and patted his hand. " It's very hot," she said. " Let's go and have an ice—a strawberry one with vanilla all round."

Now if there was one thing that the King liked more than another, it was an ice. He was always in a good temper when he was eating ices, and he ate a great many. So he stopped frowning, took the Queen's arm, and went down the High Street to the ice-cream shop.

That night the councillors came to the Queen and warned her that if King Bom interfered any more they would put him on the non-stop train to Topsy-Turvy Land, and that would be the end of *him*.

"Your Majesty, we are very sorry," said the chief councillor to the Queen, "we are devoted to *you*—and if you liked to stay behind and rule us whilst the King goes to Topsy-Turvy Land we shall be delighted."

"Oh, dear me, no, I couldn't do that," said the Queen. "I should have to go with the King if he went. If I didn't he would do all sorts of dreadful things—put his socks on inside out and try to eat his egg with a fork instead of a spoon. Things like that. I couldn't stay behind and rule you."

"Well, we don't know who else to have," said the chief councillor. "There's nobody quite so clever as you are, Queen Prylla. Just think about it, will you?"

Off they went and left the poor Queen in a great way. It would be dreadful to have to leave the Palace and go off to Topsy-Turvy Land—especially as she had only just finished making her new strawberry jam. It would be a pity to leave that before she had tasted it properly.

Queen Prylla sat and thought hard. She was fond of King Bom, for all his stupid ways, and she wanted him to be happy—but *she* wanted to be happy too, and she wanted the people to be happy as well. It was all very difficult.

"Bom would be perfectly happy if only he could sit all day eating ices!" she thought. And then a great idea flashed into her head! Perhaps she could find a way out of her difficulty, after all!

She put on a dark cloak and ran down to the ice-cream shop. It was kept by two brownies. They were most surprised to see the Queen.

"Listen," she said to them. "Tomorrow is the King's birthday, as you know. Now I want you to make a very, very special ice indeed—one that he will think is the most deliciout ice he has ever eaten. Put all the loveliest things you know into it—silver moonlight, a butterfly's blue shadow, the heart of a crocus—and flavour it with strawberry, because that is his favourite."

"Oh, certainly, Your Majesty!" said the brownies, bowing. "We will do our very best."

"Bring it up to me at eleven o'clock in the morning," said the Queen. "Don't forget."

Off she went—and this time she disappeared into a tiny

cottage at the very end of the village. Here lived Mrs. Wrinkle, a witch who had long since retired from business, and had taken up knitting.

She was pleased to see the Queen, and when she heard that she wanted a wishing-spell she was only too delighted to give her one. She still had a few left in a tin in the kitchen.

"Here's quite a good one," she said to the Queen, handing her a very small object indeed. "This will melt if you put it into a cake, for instance."

"Ah, that will do nicely," said the Queen, and she slipped it into her bag. "Thank you so much. Now pray get on with your knitting, Mrs. Wrinkle, and don't mention to anyone that I've been here."

The next day, at eleven o'clock, the ice-cream brownies arrived with the ice. It was magnificent. It was all colours of the rainbow and it glittered and shone in a most gorgeous way. It really looked far too good to eat.

The Queen took it and thanked them. Then she went quickly into the pantry with it, and slipped into the very middle of it the wishing-spell she had got from Mrs. Wrinkle.

The King had been very stupid that morning. He had sent for his councillors and given them all a good scolding, so that they fumed and raged. They went out of the Palace and came back with a large ticket.

The Queen caught sight of it as she came out of the pantry with the ice.

"Goodness!" she said, nearly dropping the ice, "is that a ticket to Topsy-Turvy Land?"

"Yes, and it isn't a return-ticket, either!" said the chief councillor angrily.

"Wait a minute!" begged the Queen. "Wait a minute! Don't be in such a hurry! I've got an idea to put everything right. Just let me try it, before you go in and give the King that ticket."

"All right," said the councillor gruffly. "But don't be long, Your Majesty."

The Queen hurried into the King's study. Bom sat there looking as black as a thunder-cloud.

"Look, Bom, dear!" said Queen Prylla, going up to him. "Here's a most delicious birthday ice, specially made for you by the ice-cream brownies."

"I don't want it," said Bom, peevishly.

"Oh, yes you do!" said the Queen, setting it down in front of him.

"Oh, no I don't," said Bom, pushing it away.

"Then I'll give it to the cat," said the Queen. "Puss, puss, puss, where are you? Come along, here's a lovely ice for you!"

"Don't give my ice to that wretched cat!" said the King crossly.

"But you said you didn't want it," said the artful Queen. "Puss, puss!"

"Well, I *do* want it!" cried Bom in a temper, and he took up the spoon and began to eat the ice.

It really was a marvellous ice. I couldn't tell you all that was in it, but it tasted like sunshine and snow, and made the King feel better than he had done for days.

"This is a very good ice," he said, when he was half-way

through. "It's perfectly delicious. The best I've ever eaten!"

The Queen watched him finish up the ice greedily. She knew that he must have eaten the little wishing-spell inside it, and she was anxiously waiting for him to say what he usually said at the end of a specially nice ice.

He said it. He finished up the last spoonful, laid down the spoon, leaned back in his chair, gave a huge sigh and said, "How I wish I could eat that ice all over again!"

Immediately his wish was granted. The ice appeared before him just as it had done when he first saw it, and in great glee he took up his spoon once more.

"Now he's off!" thought the Queen in delight. "He'll wish the wish again when he comes to the end, and eat yet another ice—and then wish the wish again. Well, he's happy for the day. Now I'll go and tell the councillors."

Off she went and told them what she had done.

The councillors peeped in at the King gobbling up his birthday ice. He came to the end and sighed, "How I wish I could eat that ice all over again!" And immediately the ice reappeared, and he began to eat it greedily.

The councillors began to laugh. They thought it was funny. The Queen laughed too. The King heard them, but instead of shouting "Off with their heads!" he simply waved his spoon at them and went on with his ice.

"You're a clever woman, Your Majesty!" said the chief councillor. "We'll take this ticket to the station and get back the money for it this very minute. You shall rule us from to-day!"

Off they went, and the Queen sank down into a chair, quite exhausted. Things had really been a little too exciting the last few days. Then she heard a contented voice from the study, "How I wish I could eat that ice all over again!"

And, so people say, King Bom is still eating ices to this very day!

The Cat, the Mouse, and the Fox

ONCE upon a time a cat walked into a trap. Click! The catch of the cage sprang down, and the cat was caught. She mewed pitifully, and a little mouse heard her and came running.

"Press back the spring, little mouse," begged the cat. "Set me free, I pray you!"

"No," said the mouse. "You would eat me!"

"I give you my word that I would do no such thing," said the cat. So the little mouse pressed back the spring and out from the cage leapt the cat. She pounced at once on the mouse, and the tiny creature squeaked in fright. "You promised not to eat me if I did you a kindness."

"You were foolish to believe me," said the cat scornfully. The mouse squeaked again, and a fox who was running by paused and listened. "What is the matter?" he asked. The mouse, with many squeaks, told him all that had happened. The fox winked at the mouse, put on a most innocent look, and turned to the cat.

"Let me get this tale right," he said. "The mouse was in the trap, Cat——"

"No," said the cat, "I was in the trap."

" Sorry," said the fox. " Well, *you*, Cat, were in the trap, and I came running by———"

" No, no ! " cried the cat impatiently. " The *mouse* came running by."

" Of course," said the fox, " the trap was in the cat and the mouse came———"

" Stupid creature ! " cried the cat angrily. " Of course the trap was not in me ! I tell you *I* was in the trap."

" Pardon, pardon ! " said the fox humbly. " Do let me get it right. Now—you were in the mouse and the trap came running by———"

"Listen!" cried the cat in a rage. "Have you no ears or understanding? I was in the trap and the *mouse* came running by———"

The cat almost flew at the fox, she was in such a rage at his stupidity. Her tail swung from side to side, and she spat rudely at the innocent-looking fox opposite to her.

" Who would think anyone could be so stupid ? " she hissed. " And you are supposed to be so sharp, Fox ! Never have I met anyone so slow and dense. Listen ! *I* was in the trap and the *mouse* came running by. Surely that is easy to understand ! "

" Quite easy," said the fox, blinking his sharp eyes. " I've got it this time, Cat. The trap was in the mouse and———"

The cat stared at the fox as if she could not believe her ears. Could anyone be so stupid ? She spat again and then glared in a fury. "I will *show* you what happened," she said. " Then perhaps you will understand at last, you very stupid fox ! "

She jumped into the trap and looked out through the bars at the fox. " See," she said, " I was in the trap like this, and the mouse came running by."

" I see *now*," said the fox, and he snapped down the spring. " Thank you, Cat, for being so patient ! The mouse will *not* set you free this time. To be ungrateful to a friend is a hateful thing—think it over in peace and quiet, for you will be a long time in the trap."

Then, leaving the cat in the cage, the fox and the mouse went off together. "You will see, friend Mouse," said the fox with a grin, "that I am not half so stupid as I appear. Good-day to you, and good luck!"